Freedom Calling

A Civil War Slave Escapes by Sea

DANA VACCA

ISBN: 978-0-692-11405-6

Chapter One

Traveling South through Virginia

The Lord will fight for you, and you have only to be silent.
(Exodus 14:14)

I never considered myself as especially brave or strong of will - or even especially clever-, but since I was a child, my mama always told me to be aware of angels around me and to listen to that little voice inside me. She called it the voice of truth, and she claimed it came from Heaven. Some might say it is intuition, or serendipity or the hand of God, but somehow I have survived this much of my journey, and I'd like to think it is because of the latter.

I lay my tired body down on a bed of fallen leaves hidden beneath a copse of oaks. It was grateful for the rest, but it begged for real sleep. I was no longer the one who waits; I was the one who has acted, and I needed to push on.

For days, weeks, I have been walking, moving only by night and keeping far from the noise of Union and Confederate skirmishing. Sometimes, the sounds of guns and cannon fire vibrate the very ground beneath my feet, and my nostrils sting from the angry, acrid smell of smoke and spent gunpowder. At other times, I hear faint echoes of the battle far off in the distance. Mostly, though, as now, there is only the music of the woodland playing to a rhythm all its own. As my steps match the tempo of its dance my fatigue vanishes, and I am carried along by the cadence of its song.

The rim of the Virginia meadow abounds with trill melodies of unseen creatures and, on silent wings, the violet mist of evening flows softly from the tangled wood beyond.

Slowly, unhurried, the incoming tide of cool damp reaches forth and caresses me with fingers, feathery and light.

I let its primal earthiness, ancient and timeless, cover and possess me.

This is the magic hour when images become dusky.

Every sense is heightened, as the wildness of the night reveals itself and rises to the throne of its birthright. The power and beauty of its sovereign rule is my lifeblood. It arouses the warrior in me. As its daughter, the will to be whole, alive and free burns in my veins.

Each evening before dark, I make an entry in this journal. My one heartfelt hope remains that my mother is still alive and that, by the Grace of God, somehow, I will find her. Mama is the one reason this journal exists, as it was Mama who taught me to read and write. If this diary is found, I have either been captured or am dead. The words written upon these pages are the only marks I will leave upon this world. I hope this journal will find its way into the hands of someone who will forward it on, and I trust the reasons for my journey will be clearly understood.

The first pages of this old, leather-bound journal are written in my mother's own hand. Her entries began with the story of her first escape from the plantation - before I was born. But she had written the account much later; after she was recaptured and brought back to Shamrock Valley. Whenever she could Mama saved parts of old ledgers and paper the master asked her to burn with the trash. She snuck them back to the cabin and sewed them together to make the diary which she kept hidden in a wall of our cabin. She said she wrote it line-by-line as seldom did she have more than a few safe minutes to write.

When I was a child, Mama told me parts of these stories many times, and when she thought I was old enough, she gave me the diary for my own. They are her stories as well as mine, as it tells of how I came to be and of how I came to be the person I am. This is some of what she had written:

From Mama's Diary

Daisy's First Escape

We know that for those who love God all things work together for good. (Romans 8:28)

I snuck away one December night just after dusk. Alone, I ran through the forest as far and as fast as my legs could take me - away from Shamrock Valley Plantation. For more than a week I've been traveling north; a wayfarer, living off what the land provides. Like a wary roe deer I kept myself hidden from sight and instinctively avoided places that so much as hinted that someone had been there before. The heavy moss on north side of the tree trunks pointed my way to freedom, and the farther north I went, the colder the nights became. My only clothing was the shapeless homespun shift I was wearing and crude, worn-out, leather-soled shoes; the usual kind slaves are given to wear. From being constantly on the move, I grew more tired with each passing day, but I kept on through the night. I had to cross many more miles before I knew I was free.

The next day, at sunrise, I was weaker and shivered with cold, but inside I was on fire. Thirsty and parched, each breath burned hot in my throat. I must find water, but walking was a great effort. My legs weighed heavy from my body and my heart raced with each labored step. I was shaky and unsteady, barely able to stay on my feet. Rushing water roared; it droned louder; my ears pounded from the din. I was swimming in snowy whiteness that was moving swiftly and murmuring words I almost understood. My scorched eyes saw only white. I was blinded. I had to stop. I had to rest. Delirious with fever and exhausted, I collapsed and sickness continued to wind its gray, leaden shroud around my inert body.

I awoke after nearly five days of delirium, with no memory of how I got to this little cabin in the woods. A tiny woman with grey hair, pulled tightly behind her head, was seated beside my bed. Curls of thin-white smoke that had a pungent but pleasant aroma, drifted from the small tin box she held in her hand. When she realized my eyes had opened, her small round face beamed. She took the pillow from her chair and put it behind me to raise my head and handed me a cup of slightly-warm, yellow tea that had been sitting on the nightstand. The sound of her voice was relaxed and soothing as she told me how she found me near a stream, deep in the valley, where she was gathering herbs. She had fashioned a makeshift pole drag that she tied to her mule and, after struggling for some time to position my motionless body on the wooden litter, she took me home. She explained how she had been doctoring me with a special home-made elixir she brewed from boneset, elderflower leaves and white willow, and between regular doses, she fed me spoonfuls of yarrow tea.

Ada lived alone in the log cabin, surrounded by endless piney wilderness. She told me she was a fourth-generation medicine woman and spent most of her time foraging for wild plants, roots and berries that she dried and stored in bottles shelved neatly in her kitchen. The income from her concoctions of mountain medicine provided for her needs. Whatever time was left over she spent writing or reading. Except for Sassy, her mule, her books were her most treasured possessions and occasionally she even had enough money left over to buy a new book.

Ada had quite a collection of books. She filled my long days of recovery by reading to me such books as *Jane Eyre*, Charles Dickens', *Cricket on The Hearth* and teaching me to read on my own, and then to write. When she thought I was ready, she gave me my first diary.

She said everyone should keep a diary or journal. It will surely help you write better, she said, but it's good for more than that. It helps you to understand yourself. Somehow in the process of writing, things get put into proper perspective. You don't have to write in it everyday, she said, but every now and then it can help you to reflect. She told me it was like having a best friend to visit with anytime you chose; one you could talk to about anything, and everything. After a while, that best friend turned into a cherished, wise, old friend that helped you remember where you've been and helped you to decide where it is you want to go.

As I grew stronger so did the friendship between us. Though Ada knew I was a runaway and would have to stay hidden from strangers, she made it clear that she hoped I would choose to stay. Working together, life was comfortable and easy, and for the first time I was truly happy. Later, though, I realized it would have been wiser to move on.

I spent four wonderful years with Ada and over that time, I filled a stack of diaries with my writing. We were both content and united in our cooperative existence, and I never gave a thought to leaving her. She told me I was the daughter she never had. I loved her. In Ada's world, I had found a peace and harmony I had never known.

One morning, a long-faced, rugged man on horseback came up the narrow path toward the cabin. He was riding a finely-bred horse and leading a smaller one behind him. He trotted his horse toward the front porch and savagely jerked it to a halt. He had pistols in his gun belt, a rifle in one hand and a reward poster in the other. Ada told me to stay out of sight and stay quiet. She went out to the front porch to meet him and closed the door behind her. I peeked out of a crack in the logs for a few moments and listened. The man was twitchy, impatient, with stony, hard eyes and a set jaw that said his temper had a hair trigger. He said he had been watching Ada's house closely for quite a few days. Several times, he had seen a black woman in the woods, and each time he had followed her here. He said the woman fit the description on the broadside.

She insisted that she lived alone, and had seen no one, but he called her a liar. He was clearly a man used to forcing his way through anything and having his own way. Though Ada, small and slight of stature, tried to stand her ground, he waved the poster so close to her face that she had to take a step back and in one motion, he stepped boldly onto the porch. In a loud, booming voice, laced with intimidation, he threatened to have her jailed for harboring a runaway slave. Then, wasting no more of his time, he threw Ada aside and stormed through the front door.

He searched every inch of the little house. I had been quick to hide myself far back in one of the kitchen cupboards, but eventually, he found me. He opened the door of my hiding place and yanked me out by one arm. Like a predator holding its prey in its jaws, he dragged me across the wooden floor and out into the yard. I screamed and struck out with my legs and arms trying to get away, but I was no match for the strength of such a large man. He tied me to onto the back of his pack horse and started back the way he had come.

That night, after he made camp, he tethered me to a tree and forced himself on me. He ground his heaving body into mine and covered me with his sickening stench of chewing tobacco, sour sweat and whiskey. The heavy, cloying pall smothered me until I dreaded taking another breath. He raped me each night of the seven-day trip back to Shamrock Valley. When we arrived at the plantation, he collected his bounty money from Rankin, the overseer and counting it as he walked to his horse, he left. I never knew his name.

Rankin came into the barn where he had me shackled, and he beat me hard with a buggy whip until my clothes were shreds around me. I could feel the stripes raised by the lash oozing blood down my back. Then he said he was going to make sure neither I nor anyone else forgot who it was that owned me. I belonged to Shamrock Valley just like the horses and the cattle. He took the hot branding iron from a bucket of hot coals he had left smoldering outside and seared the glowing shamrock iron into the right side of my face. Scorching pain shot through me, and the smokey char of my own burning flesh made my stomach wretch. Everything went black. As I slumped to the ground I heard Rankin say I was nothing more than a dumb animal, and he rightfully had dominion over all animals of Shamrock Valley. For the rest of my days, my face will carry the raised, red scar, the mark of ownership - a shamrock with an S in the center just as the branding iron left it.

Later that year, I gave birth to Celia. My first baby had been a boy, too tiny and weak to survive, and had died shortly after birth. But Celia arrived strong and healthy and very light-skinned, but she was mine; all mine. My hatred of Rankin festered deep inside and, though I knew I'd be sinning against the Lord, even killing him would not be enough to quench my simmering rage. Inwardly and outwardly, I had changed into someone I no longer recognized, but my love for Celia was my oasis from my seething fury. Having her to love was a much welcomed counterbalance to my inner torment and a much needed antidote for the vengeful poison I harbored inside. She burst my heart with a pure joy. She filled my emptiness to overflowing. I found a renewed purpose far beyond the scope of my own hurt and the monotony of my daily drudgery.

When Celia was old enough to keep it secret, I taught her letters of the alphabet by drawing them in the fireplace ash, just the way Ada had taught me. I would recite the sounds of the letters, and she would repeat them. Later, whenever we were alone out behind the kitchen garden or boiling sheets in the big cauldron far beyond the yard, I taught Celia to put the letters together to form words. Far from prying eyes she learned to sound out the words I scratched into the dirt. Soon she was able to read and write them for herself.

One day, Rankin spied on us in the garden and caught us drawing letters into words. He flew out from behind the fence hollering like a madman.

"You ain't going to be getting uppity again, ever. I guess you didn't learn who was boss well enough the first time, but I got a lesson you ain't never going to forget!"

He yanked me by the arm with such force I lost my footing and slid to the ground shrieking. Quick as lightning, he took his knife from the sheath on his belt, forced my mouth open with his grimy fingers and with one quick swipe cut out my tongue. My screams turned to gurgling as the blood gushed down my throat and out from the sides of my mouth. It poured crimson into the dusty dirt as I stared at the remnant of flesh that lay beside me like a scrap of meat cast off for cur dogs to scavenge. Rankin reached for the handle of the hot poker that sat in the fire beneath the cauldron and seared the bleeding stump.

"I ain't a-going to kill ya 'cause even like y' are, ya're still worth a whole lot more money 'n a good horse; but one way or t'other, you gonna learn yo' place. Yo' useless pickaninny kid'll get it next if I ever catch either of ya' readin' or writin' ag'in."

Inside my head, invisible hammers struck deafening blows that exploded and spread into rings of crystalline blue. Icy waves of pain threatened to drown me as they crested with each excruciating breath. Celia later told me, after Rankin turned and left, I lay so still she feared I was near death. I awoke to her sobbing over me. She stroked my face while her other hand held mine tightly. I groaned her name, unintelligibly, and saw her young face, strained in anguish, looking down at me. I cried from a pain, not of the body, but a different pain, more appalling.

I had to face that I am helpless to shield my little girl from this perverted world, where humanity is without humanity. And worse, I knew this would be her world, too. I wished that she could have

11

known only good, but sadly, that is impossible and would make little sense, here, where she must learn to vigilantly protect herself from all kinds of iniquity. But most, tragic, is that this world will be her world, as well as mine. I so regret that she had to see such harrowing villainy but, I thank the Lord, Rankin didn't harm my little girl. I pray Celia's body never feels the cruelty I have witnessed and endured.

My faith in God was all that kept me from dwelling on my past and being overtaken with anger and bitterness. Everyday, I prayed for the Lord to keep me from falling victim to the fistulous hate that threatened to eat away my heart and soul. Everyday He helped me stop it from rising like a festering cancer anxious to rot me from the inside, out. I vowed I would not be broken nor will I hold onto my pain like some whose identity is their brokenness. That would only doom Celia and me, both, forever. Slowly, very slowly, He turned my face to look with hope to the future. As iron is tempered by fire, my trials have only further strengthened my will. They have empowered me with the courage and patience to seek a better, peaceful and happy life for us.

From Mama's Diary

The Overseer of Shamrock Valley

Do not use your freedom as a covering for evil, and do not turn your freedom into an opportunity for the indulgence of the flesh; but use it as bond slaves of God. (1Peter 2:16)

Last week, very late at night, I saw Rankin, the overseer, again leaving Jennie's cabin that sits just behind ours. For some time I suspected she was a favorite dalliance of his especially after I saw his wife, Betsy, several times trailing him in the shadows right to Jennie's door. Betsy is well aware of his secret, though she'd never confront him. Even if she did, it wouldn't change anything, anyhow.

Jennie is a young house servant who was recently married to a field hand named Fred. Rankin saw to it that Fred was included in the last group of slaves that went to auction. He was taken to a plantation a few miles away, and whenever she thinks she won't be missed, Jennie sneaks away to see him. She had been missing for more than a day, and yesterday Rankin visited the big house and her cabin a half-dozen times, searching for her. She returned of her own accord, this morning. I knew there would be hell to pay.

This afternoon, Rankin had her bound, hands and feet, stripped naked and strung high up on the whipping post that stands tall in the middle of the slave yard. The Master ordered that she be given thirty-nine lashes and being well aware of Rankin's heavy hand, he seated himself on a bench beside the whipping platform to see that she got just that. Rankin laid into her hard with his full force behind every searing stroke. By the twentieth, she just hung limply by her wrists.

Blood ran red down her bare buttocks from the gashes that had been laid open on her bare back and shoulders. Her body shook with each successive flail of the rawhide as she buried her face against the rough wooden stanchion to muffle her cries. The Master sat watching without sympathy or concern. Rankin's wife, Betsy, stood looking out from the doorway of her cottage with a look, you might say, of satisfaction for the abuse being done to the object of her husband's lust. Rankin's and the Master's white children were playing marbles beside the barn and were looking on with casual interest, seemingly unaffected by the gore. They have all been witness to similar acts of cruelty before.

Rankin is a tall, thin, wiry man with a sharp, hawkish beak of a nose and a prominent chin of sparse, yellow whiskers. His small, weak eyes are squinting black slits under the wide brim of his dusty hat, but you feel their venom when he aims them your way and they spew you with disgust and contempt. He struts the slave sheds with the pluck of a barnyard bantam - his chest thrown out as if to impress. He is ever ready to strike out with his threatening tools of brutality and abuse. I've heard the sickening crack of his horsewhip echo from the fields, and demeaning, caustic shouting vomit from his pinched, taut mouth. His vulturous neck, flexing and bobbing as if performing some deranged courtship ritual, he gyrates frantically, wanting desperately what he knows he can never have: respect. Not from those beneath him in status, nor from the elite above him. He is wholly despised by the former and spurned by the latter - scorned by both.

Last week, one of the field hands told me that during the three days of the tobacco harvest, Rankin repeatedly caned Jubal, who was usually a good worker, for loading the wagon too slowly. Weak and drawn, Jubal's feverish body was moving as fast as he could manage. Rankin, figuring he was feigning sickness, ignored his pleas and mercilessly continued spurring him to step livelier and work faster. By the third day, Jubal was too sick to protest and the next morning, he was found dead in his cabin.

Yesterday, I overheard the Master berating Rankin for killing a valuable slave which, he stressed, was worth more than a year of any overseer's salary, but that just fueled Rankin's acid bitterness which he later released on the servant children. He lined them up behind the chicken coops and thrashed them with a tied-bundle of birch branches until they quaked with terror and wet themselves from fear. He told them he had to teach them who was boss now, in order to save him the trouble of doing it when they are grown. He often cuffed and flogged the Negro children, without conscience or reason. He doesn't consider them human and, I presume, the many half-Negro children he's fathered at Shamrock Valley, (the resemblance to him is unmistakable), he considers to be just half-human.

You would think under that gaunt, harsh exterior, Rankin had not any capacity for love at all, but immediately afterward, I saw him call his own white children to him. He scooped them up in his arms, affectionately and, while laughing and carrying on, went off with them to the side yard to play Game of Graces. Though with each passing year, I notice Rankin's daughter, Margaret, losing a little more of her innocence. She often cringes and turns away from her father's paternal embrace and shrinks from his bear hugs as her distaste for his wickedness deepens to hatred. I have also observed those same sons, of the Master and Rankin, chasing their young Negro playmates with hickory switches when one of them does something to displease them. Upon catching one, they strike their blows while yelling "you must be taught to obey." How else would children react to seeing the violence wrought by the hands of their fathers? Boys learn to imitate, while girls learn to fear and hate. And only God knows what other twisted, depraved persuasions might next get a foothold in these still impressionable minds.

Some have said the evils of slavery are more of a curse to the slaveholder than to the slave. I don't know that anything is worse to a slave than to be enslaved, and I carry abominable scars to prove it.

To slaveholders, though, slavery is likely a road straight to hell. It is a practice that brings out the devil in a person and gives the demons of darkness free rein to work their demoralizing and god-less wiles. I have been witness to that, with my own eyes. Master Connor has not escaped corruption, and for that matter, I have seen evil spit from the Missus, as well. But it is Rankin who can wreak the most horrible carnage and inflict the most atrocious punishment. At times, I swear, he is possessed by Satan himself.

It seems being able to dominate someone brings out a person's basest behavior and gives them the freedom to satisfy every conceivable sordid appetite of the flesh. Wielding authority can be very seductive, and a slaveholder can very easily become drunk with that kind of power. He loses all sense of right and wrong and causes suffering for all those around him. It becomes justifiable for him to beat, or even kill, anyone or anything. It becomes acceptable to rape or couple with anyone he pleases, father children with many different women, and have those children be walking testament to his immorality and evil-doings. It is acceptable to him to see the seed of his own loins enslaved and to regard them as nothing more than chattel; and just as easy for him to send them off to be sold to the highest bidder. He also has complete domination over his own wife who can do nothing but turn a blind eye and suffer in painful silence.

Dear Lord, slavery can insidiously destroy morality within a marriage, within a household or, God help us, within the entire society. Before it is too late, please bring onto us your sacred fiftieth year, your Year of Jubilee. Let THIS be that holy year of celebration when all is forgiven, all debts considered paid, and all men will be set free.

Chapter Two

Celia Heading South

Ask, and it shall be given you; seek, and ye shall find; knock, and it shall be opened unto you. (Matthew 7:7)

I walked to the edge of the clearing with the safety of full dark concealing me. Beyond, the shadowy outline a big plantation house loomed pale and gray against the deep purple of the night. At first glance, the mansion sported its expected grand splendor, but small, tell-tale signs alluded to its decline and decay. Broken fences were left un-mended, most of the livestock pens were empty, and permeating the air was the distinct and foul smell from the rotting cotton bales stacked high in open sheds and abandoned in fields. Though the fighting was not yet near, the war had ground all activity to a halt.

Closer, but off to the left, behind the mansion, stood a small building much like the little house at Shamrock Valley where Mama and I lived with the other house slaves. A tall figure slowly approached the cabin: - a Negro woman, her face lit by the lantern she carried. A large bundle was tucked under her arm. She moved towards the door of the shack, then disappeared inside. Motionless, I continued watching. Seeing no other activity for a long time, I quietly hurried across the thinly treed field to the closest side of the cabin and crouched below an open window to listen and peek.

Silverware clinked against plates. A distinct and delicious aroma of fat back and cowpeas wafted from a small open pot and mixed with the smell of fresh baked cornpone. It made my mouth water. After days of foraging for roots and berries and only occasionally snaring an unsuspecting wild rabbit or bird, this soup smelled simply heavenly - just like Mama's home-cooking. Three slaves, seated around a wooden table, passed around bowls of the hot stew, and each took a biscuit from a flat tin pan that was in the center of the table.

"The missus was besides herself today," says an older woman to the others at the table. "Mr. Dowd rode over this morning, but still no word about Master MacKenna or James, Jr. He saying there's Union soldiers down nearly to Culpepper. I overheard him say that Mr. Lincoln think he order'd all Virginia slaves to be declared free but the Confederacy still ain't never goin' t' abide by that."

"Maybe we run and make it to where them Yankees're camped; maybe they free us," said a young, strong looking, Negro man.

"You do and you won't get far before you're on the wrong end of a rope," answered an old man with silver in his hair and beard. "Tom Nolan says any slave tries to run is gonna be lynched on th' spot. I hear a few already been caught and strung up. We best stay put unless that Yankee army come here to take us away themselves."

"Been over a month or more since Lem run away. He headed for the Swamp. And Cal, then Hank, a few weeks 'afore that. I don't blame 'em for not trusting any Yankee to save their hides," the old woman added, "but even so, I say what they did was foolhardy an' plain reckless."

"There's tales about that Swamp that say hund'eds of runaways are livin' there, been so as far back as anyone can recollect" said the younger man.

18

"But remember, they weren't even sure of its exact whereabouts an' might never 've found it. An' even if they did, they never see their family or kinfolk agin," answered the old man.

"Son, just get that fool idea outta your head," the old woman went on. "No mother'd want to go on livin' not knowin' where her boy was; or if he was alive or dead!"

"I reckon you're right," the younger man answered as brightness left his face and he lowered his eyes down to stare into his bowl. "That would be a sad state; a sad, sad state, indeed."

"Only the Good Lord knows where they at now," the old man added.

I strained to listen. I was anxious to learn more about this Swamp, but they turned their attention back to eating and made no more comment. I thought to myself, with the strong family bonds of these folks, they might understand my dedication to my quest. As house slaves are usually within earshot of gossip in the big house, they may even have overheard talk about my mother or possibly some other valuable information. I slowly stood upright with my head just above the wooden sill. Gently, I knocked on the window frame. I looked directly into the eyes of the old woman and spoke hoarsely but loud enough for her to hear.

"Please! Please, help me."

The old woman looked hard at me through the open window, and said in a firm but soft half-whisper, "Who's out there?"

"I've come a long way; searching for my mama. Please, help me?" I whispered back.

"My Lord, look at you," the woman said as she scrutinized my clothing. Her dress, like mine, was the usual plain, coarse, cotton shift given to house servants, but my dress was mud stained, and so worn from dragging the underbrush, the hem was frayed to above my knees.

"I don't know what help we can be to ya', but come in by the door 'fore somebody sees ya'. And don't make no noise," she said low and hurried, and pointed toward the door.

I slipped inside. In the dim light I saw three dark figures all with eyes fixed hard on me like a pack of hunting dogs that are focused on their quarry, and waiting for it to make a move.

"You cain't be stayin' long or we'll all be in for trouble," the man said with concern for their safety. He stepped forward, cautiously but with confidence boosted by the old woman's acceptance of my presence. All three listened closely as I described Mama and her unmistakable marks.

"We ain't heard of any woman runaway slave being seen or captured, and no talk of anabody like that, anahow," the man said, "but you best be hidin' out. They hang you from the nearest tree if anybody catch you running loose around these parts." he continued. His eyes widened with fear as he spoke. I had witnessed/seen that kind of fear many times before - in the frightened eyes of a snared rabbit just before I broke its neck, or the fear in Mama's eyes anytime the overseer came around.

I stood with my oilcloth pouch containing my diary clutched close to my chest. I was uneasy, too.

"What've you got there," the younger man said to me - indicating my sack.

"Just a few of my belongings," I said and held it tighter to my chest. I was unaware that the tie had loosened, and my diary fell onto the dirt floor.

"It's a book," the old man said.

"It's my journal," I replied as I quickly grabbed it from the floor. "Every so often I write a few lines about where I've been and what I've seen."

The younger man was fascinated by the diary and asked me open it. He looked at the handwritten pages and pencil with reverence as if they were the most precious objects he had ever seen.

Then he asked, "How'd you learn to read 'n write?"

I started to speak. Nervous and stammering, I answered that my mama had taught me,... though she paid a heavy price.

"The master's childr'n got readin' and writin' books but we never allow'd in when they're gettin' their lessons," the boy replied. "It'd be an amazin' thing to be able to read what all those black marks say. But it ain't worth that kind of a whooping." He stepped back and I slid the book back into my pouch.

"You think your mama be somewhere around here?" the man asked.

I explained that Mama and I had gotten separated after running away from Shamrock Valley in White Oak. I continued on about my long journey and the other inquiries I made trying to locate her. But I found not even a clue. I told them she was the only family I had in the world. But their answers were the same. No one here had heard of Mama. Unable to hide neither my sadness nor my hopelessness, I broke down in tears of desperation and sputtered how difficult it was to admit that Mama may have been captured by Confederates, or a slave hunter, or could be dead.

The guarded expressions of the three relaxed into genuine sympathy, and the old woman came to me with arms outstretched to comfort me in her embrace.

"You poor chile," she said. "Shhh, shhhh, don't you cry, now. I'll bet your mama's probably trying to find you, too." Her arms went around me and she patted my shoulders.

For a few moments, I was in my own mama's arms, and the memory of her tugged at my heart like a thread pulled from the weave of a cloth.

It took me back to the ordinariness of days when she was always beside me - ready with her support and advice. That time seemed so far away, and so long ago.

Nurse, teacher, confidant, guide, intercessor, protector and nurturer.... Mama was all that to me. She has always been my hero. She carried me in her womb for a time, but has carried me in her heart for far longer. She taught me how to pray, to sew, to plant, to cook. When I was sick she doctored me and never left my side. It's not out of duty, though, that I must find her, nor because of our blood ties. It is love and trust that has bound us as comrades in a world where that is rare commodity.

I have prayed every night that she is still alive and free, and I am holding on with hope that we will be rejoined to share wonderful possibilities yet to come. That is what drives my journey into the unknown.

"Chile, you look half-starved," said the old woman. "I think I can do a little somethin' 'bout that!"

She motioned for me to sit, and went to the pot to spoon a bit of the beans and rice into a bowl. She placed the bowl and two pieces of warm, golden cornbread in front of me.

My eyes betrayed my hunger. I thanked her, and quickly took a seat. I put the bowl to my lips and greedily shoveled the soup into my mouth.

Between mouthfuls, I asked, "From outside the window I heard you mention the Swamp and it being a place for runaway slaves to hide out." With chunks of the cornpone I wiped the bowl clean until not a morsel remained.

"Yeah, maybe your mama's hiding out in the Dismal Swamp. I hear tell it's part of the underground to get runaways up to the north to freedom, but some just stay there to live," the younger man said while I scooped up the last of my beans.

"They's called maroons; some calls 'em outliers," the older man said as he stood up from his chair.

"How would I find the Swamp?" I searched their faces one by one.

"Cain't say for sure", the old woman said, "but most say if you head toward the risin' sun then travel a bit to the south you should come upon it. But I hear that's rough country out thatta way. Over a million acres full of gators and you got to watch your every step for poison cottonmouths and rattlers as big as your arm."

"And the air…, thick with bugs. Enough to stop up your nostrils," the boy added.

The old man got more edgy and kept glancing out the front window; then said,

"Wherever you're headed, I'm afraid you best be gettin' on your way. I beg ya'. It just ain't safe for us to have you stayin' here ana longer," he added kindly as he wrapped what was left of the biscuits in a piece of white cloth and added a chunk of pork fat from the pantry box.

He knotted the fabric neatly.

"But here, you take these along. It ain't much but the storehouse is near empty. Godspeed and may the good Lord save us all," he said as he offered the small bundle to me.

I took it gratefully and thanked them for their help then made my way out the darkened doorway and into the cool, moonless night. I headed east. I was going to find the Swamp.

Chapter Three

*Every valley shall be exalted, and every mountain and hill shall
be made low: and the crooked shall be made straight and the
rough places plain: And the glory of the Lord shall be revealed,
for the mouth of the Lord hath spoken it.* (Isaiah 40:4-5)

All through the night I traveled an un-blazed trail, bypassing roads
and looping my way around farms. I kept myself invisible and left
no trace of my presence.

In the half-light of morning I rested in a small vale. A doe raised
her tawny head above the veil of low morning mist, and her little,
spotted fawn bounded to the safety her side. She nudged the baby
with her muzzle then turned to face me. Her black nose, glisten-
ing wet and twitching; her nostrils flaring. Smelling my scent, she
was unsure. Her large ears, finely edged with black - listening and
alert. Her elegant eyes, pools of liquid obsidian, watching; spar-
kling brightly in the thin, pale light of the new day. An elegant
golden goddess of the woods, her innate urge to flee battled with
her instinct to protect and stand her ground. But the nurture in
her heart won out and put braveness in her stance. She stood more
erect, bolder, her body shielding the frightened little one pressed
close to her flank. The conflict resolved, and gallantly, she stepped
once, toward me. Her daring announced her choice to defend.
Valiant, defiant, willing to risk herself for her beloved. Soaring

high above, a hawk screamed. I glanced up just for an instant, then looked again to the doe and fawn, but they had vanished like spirits into the gray dawn.

I lay back beneath the canopy of rambling vines and fell asleep.

But let all those that put their trust in Thee rejoice: let them ever shout for joy, because Thou hast defendest them. (Psalm 5:11).

It's been three days, now, since I left the McKenna plantation behind. I crawled out from my shallow but hidden retreat where I had slept most of the day, and found there was still one of the corn biscuits left in my sack. I broke it in half and savored each morsel. With the setting sun directly at my back I started again, east, through a phantasmagorical forest that was blushed pink by the queer light that tints the end of day. During the night, I crossed many creeks which provided me clear drinking water, but there has not been, yet, any sign of a lake or swamp bog. The going was easy. The land was dry and firm underfoot, and I spent another night threading my way toward the Swamp.

The sky lightened, and the first sliver of gold glinted thinly above the horizon. I found a niche in a shady deadfall of downed logs and lay down, briefly, to ease my tired body. The coolness of the hollow reenergized me, and my newfound hope, that Mama may have found refuge in the Swamp, renewed my purpose. I was eager to be on the move again. I gathered my few belongings and went to the edge of the creek for a few handfuls of water. Leaves rustled behind me. Right away I turned to run, but I found myself looking down the long barrel of a gun.

In the next instant, the gun flashed with the loud crack of a rifle, and the shot whizzed by my ear. I ran behind the trunk of a tree and heard something slump down through the underbrush. For some moments I held my breath. I was terrified. Suddenly an arm grabbed me firmly from behind, and a hand quickly covered my mouth. A man whispered for me to keep silent as he lowered me to sit on a rock. He didn't move at all, but listened intently.

When he was satisfied there were no other sounds from the brush, he stood and said, "You best be more careful. You were about to be shot by a Reb."

The man released me, and I sat for a moment, trying to recover from the shock - my knees still weak and shaking. Then I blurted out, "It happened so fast! I thought you were going to shoot me,... but instead you saved my life!"

The tall brown-skinned man had long, coarse and straight, silver hair tied back with cord and wore leather leggings and a tan buckskin shirt. He motioned for me to follow him in the direction of where he had aimed his gun. There lay a dead Confederate soldier - a young bearded man with a bullet hole that had oozed into a spreading crimson bullseye in the center of his gray army jacket. The sight of the crumpled, bloody dead man was distressing but I directed my full attention to the strange man whose intentions were still unclear to me.

"You a Yankee?" I asked, wondering why he would rather that I was alive instead of the Rebel soldier.

I had only ever seen one Indian.... a slave at the plantation. He was just a boy and before long he was sold off to a slave dealer. But Mama told me stories about Indians that she remembered from the books she had read when she lived with Ada. This Indian resembled her descriptions but his dress and his speech was more like that of a white man. He was old, judging by the lines and creases in his brown face and his mane of nearly platinum hair, but his build was strong and his shoulders broad.

"I don't exactly side with the Union, but I sure ain't no friend to Graycoats. I was almost made a slave once, myself - a long time ago. I escaped capture but my brother didn't. He was shot in the back by a local sheriff when he tried to escape."

The Indian took the soldier's gun and ammo and offered me the dead man's Bowie knife and canteen.

"Leave the rest for the coyotes," he said. "His clothes are probably crawling with lice anyway. But you might want to take his boots. Looks like there's not much left to the soles of those brogans you're wearing."

He removed the man's boots and held them out to me. I took them and tucked them under my arm with the canteen.

He had just killed a man but his manner was gentle, and his dark eyes, clear and kind. Nevertheless, I was unwilling to trust the intentions of a stranger, even one that saved my life.

"We'd best not stay around here too long. That Reb was probably a picket scout, and more Greycoats will probably be coming this way soon. Which direction you headed?" he added matter-of-factly.

"Uh, I'm going west; back to the plantation," I lied. Cautiously I concealed the truth of my presence by pretending I was just out foraging.

"I was catching some crawdads," I added, and gestured to my oilcloth pouch hoping it would pass for a cache of the mudbugs, "I should be getting on home."

"Well, I'm going east. My wagon's just beyond that grove of trees." He paused and eyed me a little suspiciously, but bid me farewell and went on his way.

I turned westward and quickly hurried out of sight. After dark

I slipped my feet into the newly acquired leather boots. I hid the shoes in the crevice of a rotted tree and started eastward again.

Each hot day blended into the next hotter one, and I tired more easily. The shade of green forest thickets made daytime naps bearable, but even the evening air was heavy, humid and still. Sometimes I heard rumblings like distant thunder, and hours later a smokey haze from spent gun powder and burnt timber moved in and hung above the trees. I kept away from the flares that flashed from across the hills, but the raspy bite of the settling ash constantly scratched at my throat.

My wide detour away from the skirmishing took me within view of a swath of devastation that was in startling contrast to the rest of the terrain I had traversed. The countryside was an Armageddon, - bruised, battle-scourged, and scarred in the wake of cannon and musket fire. Trees were left shredded. Everywhere, downed timber lay askew, and the ground was gouged with craters and deep-cut trenches that looked like Satan's fury had exploded from the underworld below.

From afar, I spotted stiff, swollen carcasses of dead cavalry horses that perished where they had fallen. Alongside some, were smaller, less-discernible shapes, some dark, some light, a few blue, most grey, - the bodies of slain riders or foot soldiers who had stopped each other's breath; - smothered each other's voices. Scavenging buzzards squawked and squabbled as, hunch-shouldered, they coveted their positions on the corpses and greedily plunged sharp beaks into the carrion. Even from a distance, the noxious stench from the bloated, decomposing remains sickened me.

Beyond the rise of the hill, a horse and wagon had halted. Like a voyeur, I looked on as a man and woman stepped from the wagon. The woman ran to one of the prostrate forms. Kneeling in the dirt, she slumped over the dead body. The man stood solemnly behind her. I was out of earshot, but it was evident the woman was weeping inconsolably.

The man removed his hat, - his posture looked suddenly haggard and hollow; his head stooped in despair. He put a hand on the woman's shoulder; to console her and possibly to steady himself. Seeking relief from her anguish, she reached back and grabbed his arm. Distraught, they stayed that way as if touching each other would dull their agony; - both desperate to dilute the pain that wracked their hearts.

The verdant landscape was no longer a place of life. It was a place of slaughter. The savagery of mankind had been laid out in the harsh, cruel light of day and had yielded a harvest of death.

The rupture between the warring sides yawned wider. The South, jealous of its rights, fought for state independence and slavery. Negroes risked their lives for personal independence. The North fought for unity and freedom for all. Yankees, Confederates, Negroes - died for their beliefs. Some killed neighbors, friends, brothers for what they believed to be right and just. Slaves killed masters for what *they* believed to be right and just. Who should be called savages? All of them? None of them? I kept among the trees and hurried past, but the carnage of the life-less battlefield haunted me miles after I had left it behind.

Except for an occasional grassy plain, the land had become unre-markable, and showed no sign that I was nearing my destination. The weariness I had staved off now began to take hold of me. Lone-liness and anticipation kept urging me on, but I felt abandoned and betrayed by the universe - overcome by emptiness and desolation. I envisioned dozens of possible endings to my journey as I walked. Some "what if"s concluded joyously and others, full of sorrow. In spite of my persistence and willingness to face any obstacle, inside me grew a gnawing fear that eroded my hope like lapping waves on a sandy bank…. Finding Mama might not be possible.

You, dear diary, have been my only source of companionship, and writing, my only form of expression. I didn't dare even risk talking to myself as I walked. Instead, in my head, I hummed songs that no one else could hear. At first, the lyrics were often melancholy and full of gloom.

> Sometimes I feel like a motherless child,
> A long way from home.
> Sometimes I feel like I'm almost gone,
> I wonder where my mother has gone.
> I'm troubled, I'm troubled in my mind.
> If Jesus don't help me
> I will surely die.

But somehow the music that played inside me changed and slowly lifted my spirits, and my silent humming transformed into a hap-pier tune. I declared to myself that I would not wallow in self-pity and I sang:

> Someone in the fiery furnace,
> And they begin to pray.
> An' the good Lord smote that fire out.
> Oh, wasn't that a Mighty Day, Lord,

Oh, wasn't that a Mighty Day.
Daniel went into the lion's den,
And he began to pray.
And the Angels of the Lord
Locked the lion's jaw.
Oh, wasn't that a Mighty Day, Lord,
Oh, wasn't that a Mighty Day.

Chapter Four

"Blessed is the one whose sin the LORD does not count against them and in whose spirit is no deceit."
(Psalm 32:2)

As dawn approached, staccatos of gunshots blasted out of the valley to the north. I crossed well beyond the next southerly ridge to avoid risking an encounter with flanking soldiers and kept moving all day through the forest to put a safe margin between me and the shooting.

I ascended a sparsely-treed hillock that was dotted with low mounds of bare earth, - not freshly turned ground, but disturbed recently enough to not yet have sprouted weeds or grown any moss. As I passed slowly, I realized these were the shallow graves of dead soldiers. Though they were nameless and unknown, this newly-dug and unmarked burial place was a sobering sight.

Further on was something even more grisly. In a sun-baked patch of darkly-stained mud lay a twisted heap of rotted clothing - blackened and defiled; and haphazardly scattered in the pile, were bones. At one end, unnaturally angled, was a pair of crusty, Army-issue boots, and at the other, was a human skull. This soldier must have died months ago, or longer, but the leathery skin and clumps of matted hair that still clung to his head made it all too shockingly clear that these remains had once been a flesh-and-blood person.

In the center of the heap, ghoulishly jutting out from what had been a jacket sleeve, was a hand that looked like an evenly-arranged row of dry, dead twigs. The top of a tiny book peeked out from under the sleeve cuff. I picked it up and opened it to where a pencil had been tucked into the pages. The paper was blood-smeared in places, but the writing was still legible. It was a letter.

Friday, March 31, 1865 near Dinwiddie, Virginia
Robert Mitchell
1st North Carolina Cavalry

My Dear Olivia,

By the time you read this you will already know of my fate. As I lay in the woods, alone, I fear I will not live to see another sunrise - for I am mortally wounded, and these may be the last words I can say to you before it is too late.

Under the command of Colonel Cheek, we dismounted near Fitzgerald's Ford and in a torrential rain, made our way across the swollen creek. The water was so deep we had to hold our rifles and ammo over our heads. We were fired on by waiting Federals while crossing and lost many men. Some of us made it up the north hill to the heavy cover of the trees, but there we were continually pelted by the gunfire of our unseen enemy. It was then that I was hit in the side by a minie ball.

Boys from the Maine regiment charged across the field towards us. Our remaining men headed out to meet them - all except for me, - and my brother. Henry knew I was seriously wounded and didn't want to leave me alone. He stayed with me a long while and made me as comfortable as he could. We heard heavy firing start up again. This time it was closer. I told him he should go in case Yankees tried to take the hill.

Livi, I have fought hard for the Confederacy and pledged

all that I am to preserve our homeland. Daily, I pray the South will be victorious. It is my firm belief that slavery is part of the Lord's ordained plan to ensure Negroes are taken care of and taught to lead good, Christian lives. Even the Holy Bible says slavery was established by decree of the Almighty God! It is for the good of all - negro and white. I wished I could have returned to you unharmed, but I do not regret giving my life to help our important cause triumph.

My only regret, my sweet, is that I must leave you now. I worry for your safety and well-being, especially if the South should lose. It sorrows me that I can no longer be with you in body to protect you from harm or misfortune - or bring happiness to your heart. Our earthly bond was not supposed to end this way, nor was it supposed to end so early when we are but in the summer of our love. But remember, my love, I will always be with you in spirit. As I write, I am holding your photograph and gazing at your lovely face. How I wish I could kiss you even just once more. Please know, my darling, that I will love you for eternity and will patiently wait for the time when we are together again.

It is late afternoon and after two days of rain, the sky is now beautiful, blue and clear, and the sun is shining brightly. I am resting on this hillside, but I am growing weaker and don't think I can write much longer. I will keep my eyes on your picture so you will be the last thing I see in this world.

Do not mourn for me, my dearest. Instead remember me in life - our life together. In unwavering faith I am prepared to meet my Savior when death takes me. And I look forward to the joyous day when we meet in Heaven and are united again.

Your loving and devoted husband,

Robbie

The letter was heart-wrenching. I closed the book and stared at the corpse, - unable to turn away from the horror of the disturbing scene. Beside the fingers I noticed another object, small and square. I picked it up and turned it over. It was a tintype case. Inside was a photograph of a beautiful, young, fair-skinned girl of about my age. It was Olivia, whose picture he so tenderly clutched as he clung to life, - until his heart could beat no more. Somewhere, she had been waiting for her beloved to return home. Somewhere, she would mourn his passing and grieve for him.

This soldier had taken lives and sacrificed his own for the sake of his beliefs. He felt so strongly for his cause that even death was not too big a price to pay to champion it. Below, the ground was covered by others who had done the same. I wondered about my own mortality, - my own attachment to life. How would my own fortitude measure against the mettle of this soldier? My desire to be free, my desire to find Mama; - I held those convictions just as deeply.

The North and South had agreed to settle the issue of slavery by placing it on trial by war. Military might would decide the winner, but how many more would die? When faced by a rifle there was little option except to shoot or be shot - kill or be killed. Like it or not, that was a grim but unequivocal fact. I remembered the Rebel who had had me in his gun-sight, and the Indian's quick shot, - the only reason I was still alive. How quickly and easily life could be extinguished, - in less than a second. I shuddered.

Even if the North won the physical battle, the differences between the Union and the Confederate attitudes were irreconcilable. Winning a war can change borders, but can it change the ideology - would losing the war change the defeated side's *way of thinking*? How could this kind of war end? Confederates were not going to cast off their Southern way of life like an old coat. For generations the South had passionately held the conviction that keeping Negroes slaves was moral, noble, Christian and lawful. The unwillingness of Confederates to grant equality to Negroes was plainly shown by the remnants of the lost lives disintegrating around me.

I was chilled by a premonition, - the sum of all fears. I placed the book and tintype case on the jacket cuff and hastened from the clearing. Once again in the denser forest, I descended lower toward the valley bottom and into the inviting shade of tall pines.

"God intended it for good to accomplish what is now being done. So don't be afraid. I will provide for you." (Genesis 50:21)

Sudden, short screeches startled me. Beside me, the scrub brush exploded with flailing wings and fluttering feathers. I crouched, and a small flock of wild turkeys rose up - just missing my head. I turned and looked expecting more to follow, then my legs turned to stone. There stood the old Indian. His bow was in hand and a quiver of arrows hung from one shoulder. Slung over the other shoulder was a large, dead turkey. An arrow still stuck through its middle.

"Hello, again, little one," he said with gentleness in his voice.

"This will make a good meal," he said holding the turkey by its feet. "Would you like to share it? No need to waste such a fine bird. It's much more than I need."

For a few moments I stared up at his face that was genuinely friendly and sincere, and into his clear, dark eyes that showed no malice.

"I sure would," I answered.

"Then follow me. I've already made camp." Assuming I was behind him, he walked along the tree line to a small, protected clearing. He had concealed his horses under the lowest drooping boughs of an old live oak. They were unharnessed and tethered so they could eat from the bunches of the gray-green Spanish Moss that heavily draped the branches. He had already gathered a pile of dry wood and sticks behind them, and a shovel leaned against one of the small logs.

"You know how to clean this?" he asked as he held the bird by its neck.

"Oh, yes," I said nodding my head. "I've done it lots of times."

"I'll dig a hole for the fire so it won't be visible to anyone, and we can cook pieces of the meat on sticks. I'll bet you're pretty hungry. I know I am, and you've been traveling on foot!" he said as he pushed on the shovel with his boot and scooped out a large clod of dirt.

By the time the turkey was cleaned and cut, the Indian had the fire going. We poked thick twigs through the pieces of meat, and hung them over the fire to cook. He watched the strips browning, and without looking up he asked, "Aren't you a long way from home, little one?"

"I kinda lost my way," I answered as I took one of the strips and bit off a big mouthful of the stringy meat.

He glanced at me for a moment then took one of the sticks and began to eat.

"You running from something or to something?" he asked.

Still chewing, I glared at him, but he was still still staring into the fire.

"You don't have to answer if you don't want to," he said. "but I thought I might help you get to where you're going," he continued. "I'm pretty good at keeping clear of trouble."

Frightened at his intent, I rose to my feet and immediately began stuffing my few belongings into my pouch along with a few of the turkey strips. I wasn't sure I should trust this man, and I wasn't willing to risk my freedom. I thanked him for the vittles and backed away - prepared to run.

He looked up at me and gestured for me to stay. "No, no!" he said. "You needn't go. I'm sorry. I didn't mean to say you'd be a cause for worry. What I meant was, I've been traveling alone a long time, and I wouldn't mind the company. I travel old Indian trails to stay out of sight and I suspect you'd probably want to do the same.

"I am called Enapay," he said. "Anpetu washte." He used the Sioux greeting. "I am happy to know you, little one."

I stopped moving and he continued speaking.

"If you're headed east, it might be safer and easier for us both if we cross this territory together, so long as you don't mind helping to gather food and firewood."

With my eyes fixed on the Indian, I stood, scrutinizing his words and trying to determine whether I should remain or flee.

"You can ride in the wagon with me or ride Ol' Beau. Either way, it'll be a lot easier than walking. It's many days journey to the swamp settlement where I do some trading. You're welcome to ride with me until then."

I considered his offer. It almost seemed too good to be true. Could he be talking about the Dismal Swamp? And would it be safe to let him help me get there, or was he just telling me what he thought I wanted to hear?

"You trade with Outliers?" I asked matter-of-factly. I didn't want to seem too eager but I wanted to know more about his connection to the swamp people. I also wanted to learn more about his character before agreeing to be travel companions.

"Yep, been running goods to and from the Dismal Swamp for a long time. The wagon and those packs on Beau are filled with things the Outliers can't make or find, like axe heads, bayonets, knives, shovel heads, matches, planting corn, and even a couple of musket rifles, though with the war raging, those are extremely hard to come by, even for me. For those things they trade me leather, gator skins, moonshine and tanned deer hides and sometimes bear, cougar, or 'coon skins."

Because the war has most of the coastline blockaded, the leather and especially the moonshine bring unheard of prices."

"What's the Swamp like?" I asked.

"One thing is, it's wild and inhospitable…, and big. It's near a million acres and nearly impenetrable in parts; except by the most hardy souls. But it's probably the best place for a runaway slave to find freedom without having to risk going north. Indians and melungeon half-breeds have been living there for a long, long time. Some live out their lives there. Others, like me, stayed for a while and then moved on."

I listened with keen interest and, noting the change in my manner, he studied me even more closely.

"I have a notion you are headed to the Dismal," he watched for my reaction, but I gave none.

"You once lived with the Maroons?" I asked.

"Sure did. You see, when my brother was shot I didn't just escape capture and run. I hid myself 'til dark, and that night I killed the man who killed my brother. So, I've got a bounty on my head, though that was a very long time ago."

"Maybe so," I commented, "but bounty or not, I wouldn't exactly call what you did cold-blooded murder; I think I'd be more inclined to call it justice."

"The law wouldn't quite see it that way, especially for an Injun," he replied.

"How did you know about the Swamp?" I said, feeling at ease to ask more questions.

"It's Indian legend. The Swamp has been a hiding place for generations. The maroons kept me safe there until enough time had passed. Then, gradually, I ventured out for short periods. Later, I made longer trips, hunting and trapping farther along the Great Path. It's an ancient Indian trail that has been used by many tribes as far back as anyone can remember. One of its many branches passes very close to the

Swamp. The game is plentiful, and I always returned with food and skins for the maroons."

"You must know that land well." I said.

"Been traveling it most of my life."

"Then what made you become a trader? Seems like an unlikely business for an Indian," I said, with half a smile as I squatted down on a log in front of the fire.

"The profession chose me more than I chose it," he said. "Every season, an Indian, a Saponi, visited the Swamp in his buckboard stacked high with dry goods, hardware, and tools. We were one of his regular stops. He was always a welcome sight. He would trade with us for pelts, leather, wild herbs; whatever we had to barter. The Saponi people were well known merchants and many ranged far beyond their native lands.

"He invited me to ride his route with him. For three seasons I went as his helper. I was young and strong. He was old and tired, and the work was becoming harder for him. On our last trip together we stopped for the night about thirty miles southeast from where we are now. He lay down on his bedroll and I on mine, and in the morning I was unable to wake him. He was dead. I put his body in a bier I fashioned out of wood from the wagon and raised it high on sturdy tree limbs. That is the Sioux custom. I placed his personal items in the box with him, and enough food to last him on his journey to the Great Spirit. "

"How sad," I said. "He must have been a good friend."

"Yes, he was - like a second father to me."

"What was his Indian name?"

"It is bad manners to speak the Indian name of the dead, but in white man's language his name was Sky Eyes. I can tell you his soul was pure, and he had no fear of death. He knew what it was to walk in the clouds, and I know his journey to the Big Sky was a peaceful one. I took over his trade, to honor his spirit, and have made his stops twice a year, ever since."

"But traveling all the time?" I interjected reflecting on all the time I had spent alone. "Wouldn't you rather return your people - the Sioux, I mean?"

"In a way, the Swamp people are my family now, and I do visit them - about three times a year. I am able to bring them many necessary things that the land can't provide them. I still visit my tribe, too, though much less often since my mother and father went to the spirit world more than two dozen years ago."

We talked for a long time. He told me that both his father and his mother were brave warriors and were highly regarded in his tribe of more than two thousand Sioux. His father was badly wounded one autumn defending their cache of winter provisions against a band of Crow who waged a particularly brutal and desperate attack to raid their stores. He died in the arms of Enapay's mother. Wanting to avenge her husband's death, his mother began riding into battle alongside the warriors of the tribe. He told me he insisted that his mother allow him to honor his father and fight in her place. She understood her son's desire to protect her and give homage to his father's memory, but she lovingly but firmly, always answered that it was her privilege to pay tribute to his spirit. She told him his duty was to bring glory to the lives of those who had rescued him from slavery - the people of the Swamp.

Enapay's mother rode her war pony into many retaliatory skirmishes and "counted coup" on dozens of Crow. She warred unharmed until her final battle when her horse was mortally wounded by a lance. She lost her shield as he fell. Left on foot, she continued fiercely wielding her spear and shouting her mighty war cry, but was fatally struck from behind by a young Crow's tomahawk.

Enapay explained the Sioux custom of cutting a gash in one's arm or leg to express grief over the loss of a loved one. He proudly showed

41

me the scars, one on each of his forearms, where he had cut himself to mourn each of his parents' deaths. There was another on his upper arm for the death of his friend, Sky Eyes and a fourth, wider and longer mark on his chest for the loss of his brother.

"However it happens, losing someone you love is hard to bear", I said solemnly as I thought of my own mother. I prayed each night for the Lord to be keeping her safe, and tears came to my eyes at the mere chance that she might be lost to me, or even worse, dead.

"I loved each of them deeply. Our souls,... bound together always", Enapay said.

"Shared hearts," I said almost to myself as if thinking out loud. "It is a rare and precious gift to live loved."

A tear spilled slowly down the right side of my face before I quickly brushed it away.

Enapay sensed my woefulness, and with quiet gentleness said,

"So tell me, little one..., where are you going?"

Something about the man made me believe he was worthy of trust, but I didn't answer him or raise my head. After much rumination and hearing him speak about his past, he had convinced me of his honesty, and I counted him forthright and true.

"Yes, Enapay," I said. "I will ride with you to the Swamp." I liked him and I forced my somber expression to soften enough to manage a weak smile.

Enapay beamed and his dark eyes smiled.

"It's late," he said, "and we should rest a while before we go on."

I agreed.

Working together in silence, we doused the fire and hid all traces of our presence. Enapay took the first watch and sat in the shadows of the hollow where we had hidden the all his gear. He handed me a bedroll which I stretched out under a low-lying pine.

I laid there for a while, on the soft, quilted blanket. I thought about the strange past of my new friend and the turn his life had taken when he was not much older than my age of eighteen. He had been suspended between two very different worlds, but he was yoked to neither. On the inside, I sensed his soul was peaceful, and content: - neither pulling nor being pulled by anything or anyone; and neither pushing nor being pushed. Instead it seemed he was balanced on the crest of the universe where, like a graceful willow, he moved in harmony to its undulating tenor and bent effortlessly to the winds of the divine.

"Enapay," I called out in a loud whisper. "If we're going to be riding together, I guess you should know my name. It's Celia."

"Celia," he repeated enunciating it slowly.

"What's your name in white man's language?" I asked.

"My name means, Appears Bravely," he answered.

"Enapay, Appears Bravely," she muttered softly.

"Ok, then Celia." He chuckled. "You should rest now. I'll wake you in a few hours."

In that ripple of thin scrim between sleep and wakefulness, I drifted. The cool autumn air whispered to me gently as I looked up at the full, yellow moon. It glowed bright and round and rose like the sun in the dark, but starry sky. *Big and bold - so near to me…*, I thought.

"My arms want to reach out to you, there, just beyond the earth's edge. I want to bathe in your golden light. There, like the moon, you are standing, and if I stay a little longer, I can feel you. If I reach just a little further, I can touch you. I know it has been a long time, though you must never think I'm not coming. I will wait, or else you will slip out of my present and into my past. But something must be wrong; I feel nothing. I must be numb. Where are you? I can't reach you, I can't feel you, or did I just imagine you were there?"

Chapter Five

*Then God said, "I give you every seed-bearing plant on the face
of the whole earth and every tree that has fruit with seed in it.
They will be yours for food.*
(Genesis 1:29)

Enapay didn't seem to need much rest, so a few hours after sundown
we set out again along a narrow grassy swath not much wider than a
foot path. We were moving deeper towards the lowlands over more
flat, even ground that was less tiring on the horses. During the day-
light hours, I rode a good distance behind the wagon so I could duck
into the brush undetected if I heard Enapay's eagle cry, the signal to
hide, but, so far, we had encountered no one. We traveled well into
the night. The air was pleasant, and the evening passed uneventfully.
Just after dawn Enapay stopped and pointed to a barely noticeable
opening in the bushes.

"Through there," he said. "There's a brook."

Again we hid the wagon. When we stopped, I took care of the
chores as I had promised, and I led the horses to the edge of the
stream to let them drink their fill. Standing in the cold, clear water
made my legs dot with gooseflesh, and the swift current tickled my
ankles when I waded in deeper to top off the canteens. After the
horses were secured Enapay pointed to some wild waterleaf that
covered a shady bog beside the riverbank. He told me to gather some

of its tender two-toned leaves and he went to pick some deep-purple black mulberries that were growing farther up the ridge. When he returned we sat with our backs against a dead tree trunk and shared our harvests along with leftover pieces of turkey that had turned dry and hard but were still edible.

"More streams and marsh now that we're in the low country," Enapay explained as he took a handful of berries. "But it is safer, using this route. White men would rather trek up and down the hills than slog through the wetlands. And there are enough hummocks in the marshes for us to find a dry camp when we need to stop."

Our pace was more leisurely now, and I tied Beau to the back of the wagon and rode on the seat, beside Enapay. We came to a low hill, thick with mounds of tall, shaggy grass that gently waved their feathery maidenheads in the October breeze. The tops had turned sandy brown, ripe and plump with seeds. Enapay stopped, and with a bucket from the wagon, he went along the edges of the reeds and shook their spiky plumes into the pail. He said when we made camp we would boil the grain like rice, until it was swollen and tender, and eat it with dinner.

Farther on, Enapay stopped at a small pond that was covered with a blanket of water lilies and lily pads so completely, that only a bit of water was visible at the middle. He sent me with a basket to pick some of the beautiful, white, cup-shaped flowers and a few handfuls of the lotus leaves. They, too, later boiled in water, were delicious. Enapay said they also made a good remedy for dysentery.

From Mama's teaching, I was already familiar with the black

willow, with its distinctive, long, cascading branches that draped towards the ground like ropy garland. Enapay cut a few low hanging boughs. A few times a day he chewed on a handful the leaves to relieve his soreness from the rough wagon ride. My absolute favorite wild find, though, was still the persimmon fruit, so sweet and delicious. It was plentiful here and just beginning to ripen.

I had a growing admiration for this man whose ancestors survived in this land for eons, and passed down their skills from one generation to the next. He was resourceful, resilient and wise without guile, and he astounded me with his knowledge of the earth's abundant bounty. Even Mama, who had learned a lot about wild herbs and medicines, would have been impressed! By the time we stopped to camp, we had enough for our meal, but Enapay never took more than we would use each day. He respected Mother Nature's generosity. He said that if we honored her and took from her only what we needed, she would always keep us in her care.

Enapay had been teaching me to shoot with his bow. I wasn't very good at it but I did improve a little with each lesson. He was a very patient teacher and I tried to be a good student. Tonight, while I was stringing the bow, a rabbit hopped out of a spicebush and stopped to nibble some grass. I took aim, confidently, and released my arrow. I watched it sail far too high above the rabbit and a little off to the right. Beside me, Enapay was grinning and trying hard not to laugh.

"Keep trying, Celia," he told me, "and do not be discouraged. It takes a lot of practice to be skillful enough to hit small game."

I could hear him chuckling as he walked off behind the wagon to roast the quail he had shot earlier. I used a rotten log for a target and fine-tuned my aim until my arms were too tired to stretch the bow. When I stowed the bow and arrows back in the wagon, I told Enapay I was glad I didn't have to rely on my own hunting ability for our supper.

The late autumn evening was clear and crisp. The nearly-full moon had begun to rise, and it cast a pearly pallor on everything but the shadows. At the rim of the forest, a great owl, the angel of the gloaming, ascended silently. Its ghostly wings, like soft, white lace, made not a whisper. Higher and higher, it floated through indigo boughs; to a unseen aerie it rose - flying; free, dissolving into the deep purple nightshade of the treetops like a supernatural apparition.

With little danger of interlopers this near to the Swamp, we were safe in this secluded grove for the entire night. The mood was almost festive as we dined on bobwhite, roasted and crispy, and feasted on the other victuals that we had in our daily store. The campfire logs crackled and glowed red below flickering yellow flames that danced in the twilight. I sat propped against my bedroll, and the heat from the fire warmed the air around me. Enapay sat opposite reclined comfortably in the curve of the pack saddle.

We sat that way for a long time and conversed, then hypnotized by the fire, became silently reflective. I was filled with a tumult of emotion partly because Enapay, so kindly and benevolent, had been such a blessing to my plight - but also because our destination was so near. Very soon my hope of finding my mother would be transformed into a reality - one of overwhelming elation or one of agonizing disappointment. I also knew the time had come to trust Enapay with my story and my true reasons for going to the Swamp.

"I want to tell you the truth about my past, Enapay," I said. "As a friend, you deserve at least that much, or more. It has been callous of me to return your openness with aloofness when you've been so honest and generous to me." I felt twinges of guilt for my evasiveness.

"I was a runaway, Enapay, ... My mama and I ran away from our plantation in White Oak. And there's a chance she made it to the Swamp."

"But when our paths first crossed you were very far to the north," Enapay said.

"Yes, we had gotten separated. I'll tell you the story from the beginning," I said.

This is how it all began. I started reading to him from my diary, and once I started talking I couldn't stop.

Chapter Six

Shamrock Valley

Ye are of God, little children, and have overcome them: because greater is He that is in you, than he that is in the world. (1 John 4:4)

The war between the North and the South had already begun, but my only real knowledge of it came from whatever information I could glean by eavesdropping in hallways, hiding in bushes or under windows and listening to the conversations of the many who came almost daily to the plantation house. I knew the Union had pushed its way deep into the South, and many of the local menfolk were away, either still fighting or else dead. But so far my life at Shamrock Valley Plantation had changed very little.

This morning Mr. Tobias Pettigrew came to call on Master Connor. He was the town clerk as well as a large plantation owner, and the Master's oldest and closest friend. I surmised this might be a good opportunity to overhear some important news. I carried the wash basin from the pantry to the porch, and Mama and I began scrubbing the porch floor near the open window of the library where we could hear the two old friends talking.

"The Union soldiers have advanced their front lines all the way down to Fredericksburg and they're enforcin' Lincoln's document that declared all slaves free. We've got to make certain the negroes don't get wind of it or we'll have hell to pay. With mostta our hired hands gone, we'd never prevent 'em from all runnin'. I've lost a few already," Tobias said angrily.

"I am not goin' to let those Yankees take my rightful property from me, and that includes all the slaves I own. We can't let Lincoln dictate how we run our farms. And I'm not abidin' by any United States ruling, because we're no longer a part of it! These slaves are my property, and I have bills of sale to prove it." The master's voice boomed loud and his temper flared.

"I'm with ya all the way, Henry. You know that. You an' I have always thought alike. And I'm not too ole yet to pick up a gun myself, if necessary, and make 'em believe we no longer pledge allegiance to the United States." Tobias went on. "We've lost so many men and boys, I might just do that before it's too late to stop them damn Yankees from overrunnin' us all."

When Mama and I were again alone I couldn't contain my excitement about the President's decree to end slavery. Mama was amused by my high spirits, but made sure she firmly impressed upon me to keep this new-found information to myself. She went on to say, that with the Union soldiers pushing further and further South, things would soon begin to change around the plantation, but probably not for the better - at least not at first. The master was a fair but stubborn man and once riled he was not easily going to let go of anything that belonged to him. Whether it was his land, his home or his slaves. He would fight hard to protect what he felt was rightfully his, and the other slaveholders will do likewise. For now, she cautioned, we best go on with daily chores just like always. I obeyed her warning, but the possibility of gaining freedom awakened a restlessness in me that I had to struggle to hide. That same glimmer of hope shed its light on Mama, too, and made her even a little more cheerful than usual.

A week or so later, Mr. Pettigrew returned, and once again he was shown to the library to converse privately with the master. Mama and I had been sweeping the porch steps when he arrived. After the front door closed behind him, we moved to sweep near the same window to listen to the latest report.

Master Connor began ranting about the terrible economic conditions. Most of the cotton and tobacco he had harvested was just sitting in the barns. and at present, he was looking financial ruin straight in the face.

"I know, I know," said Mr. Pettigrew. "This winter I've only managed to get a very small amount of my crop to market, too. Had to ship it through a small blockade running steamer that ran it to Nassau where an English contract agent handled it from there. With so many hands in the till, I got barely four cents a pound - next to nothin' for it."

"I did the same," said the Master. "but I can't keep going like this."

"That's what I came to talk to ya' about, Henry. Recently, I've gotten in on a venture you may wanna consider. You're my best friend, and we've been neighbors most of our lives," Mr. Pettigrew said. "And I wouldn't encourage you to partake if I hadn't already engaged in it myself, but first you gotta promise you won't leak a word of what I'm going to tell ya."

"Of course, Tobias. You got my solemn oath."

"A Massachusetts mill representative, Eli Robinson, came callin' last week. He told me his mill operations were almost at a standstill because of the unavailability of raw cotton, and the demand for his textiles is at an all-time high. At his wits end, he purchased a merchant ship and two of his own small steamers. The faster, low-profiled steamers have gotten cotton an' tobacco out through the blockade. Once in international waters, they discreetly met up with the larger vessel. They transferred the cargo and the loaded ship sailed back to New Bedford. Now his mills are up and runnin' again, but he needs another shipment and has offered to buy the remainder of my harvest."

"What about the Union Navy? And a merchant ship loaded with cotton headin' north and puttin' into a Union port ?… I don't know, Tobias," he shook his head. "If the cotton is found on board the boats, our crops'll be confiscated."

Tobias continued, "First, the good news. Mr. Robinson pays up front and assumes all risks. Second, he's already completed a number of shipments successfully. He claims his risk is very small. The Union has no jurisdiction in the open sea and has even been turnin' a blind eye to these clandestine dealins. There is so much profit to be made on both sides that many government officials and military men, includin' generals an' soldiers, are on the take. They're bein' bribed to shut their eyes. The mania for cotton by the factories and manufacturers has even spurred Congress to issue cotton permits, as needs warrant. President Lincoln, himself, has been unable to stop the cotton trade!"

"Yes, Tobias, that sounds more favorable, but isn't Robinson goin' to offer us just a pittance for our crop? It won't be much different than sellin' to those other double-dealin' scoundrels."

"That's just it, Henry, the best news is what they're willin' to pay. Seventy cents a pound for the cotton! Fourteen times what we have been gittin' from those other bandits we've had to do business with. And they'll pay eleven cents a pound for tobacco!"

"Indeed," said Master Connor, "that IS good news. Good news indeed!" There was a pause.

"If you're interested, there's room for twice what I'm supplyin' 'em - room for about one hundred-and-fifty more bales of cotton and thirty-five more barrels of tobacco."

"No doubt, I'm interested!" the Master answered. "Goodness, Tobias, you are a Godsend!"

"No thanks needed, Henry. Times are hard, an' we have helped each other many times in the past. Have your barrels and bales at my barns by Wednesday night. Robinson will pay for the whole shipment on Thursday, and I'll have your money by Friday at noon. The steamers are already in port. My wagons will haul the two loads down to the docks well after sunset on Friday night. The boats will be loaded quickly then they'll promptly depart."

"I'll have the shipment in your barns by tomorrow afternoon," Master Connor said to Mr. Pettigrew.

"Fine, Henry. I'll get word to Mr. Robinson that he'll have a full ship."

Mama and I were on the other side of the porch and out of sight by the time Mr. Pettigrew exited the house.

Chapter Seven

I am the LORD your God, who brought you out of the land of
Egypt, out of the house of slavery.
(Exodus 20:2)

Mama and I were both born into slavery, but to me, a life of liberty
was more a magical limbo conjured by an imagination that took me
floating far beyond the invisible walls of my confines. For Mama,
though, freedom was more than a fabrication. I was just a tot the first
time she told me of her escape to independence. Since then she has
told me many more details about that part of her life. She still calls
it "the time she ran from bondage and the Lord had let her have her
head." She reached beyond the limits imposed upon her and for a
time, knew what it was to live free.

Those years brought sharper clarity to her understanding of freedom. She taught me that being keeper of your own destiny didn't
necessarily grant you an easier life, nor one of any special privilege.
Basic needs, like keeping food on the table and a place to call home
required hard work, and a lot of it. Rewards were hard fought and
hard won. She told me she learned from experience and from her
studies with Ada, that one way or another, a person, free or not, is
always beholden to someone else, whether they're earning a daily
wage, selling wares, harvesting crops or raising livestock. And, with
human nature being what it is, every person, free or not, has some

kind of prejudice. It didn't matter who you are or where you were; like there are Southern prejudices, there are Northern prejudices, too. There's also not a soul, free or not, who has not been a victim of some type of prejudice, injustice or exploitation. Nevertheless, to a bought-and-paid-for slave who has only known legally sanctioned subjugation and tyranny, any kind of emancipation is welcomed even if it is a little slippery. Emancipation means envisioning a new and better future and opportunity to choose, to learn, to love, and to carry tomorrow in your own hands and affect whether it will be better or worse than today.

You see, even though she was captured, forced back to the plantation, and even maimed, in most ways Mama had never ceased being free and could never again truly be enslaved. Neither her mind nor her spirit will ever be owned by anyone. Tenaciously, she held on to the hope of regaining her freedom. Often, when she could still talk, she'd say, "You'll see, Celia. The good Lord is making a way for us and the time is coming soon." That dream, neatly tucked away but never waning or forgotten, had always been fueled by her undaunted will, a will so strong that she told me, when she was a child, she made up her mind that she'd grow to be six feet tall. And she did, with a half inch to spare. She raised me to believe that same kind of power coursed through my veins. I could be whatever it is I set my mind to be. A will that strong has the power to make things happen.

The rest of the day I pondered about what it would be like to be free and not live in constant fear of one of us being sold off and separated forever. The likelihood of Mama being sold had gotten greater with each year. She was growing older, less spry and never bore more babies. Despite forced couplings with field hands plainly sent to her bed by the overseer, Mama never carried another baby after me. A slave's value is measured only by productivity and usefulness and we both knew it was only a matter of time before we would be split up. There was another reason. Though she could never talk about it,

I knew Mama prayed that her wish for freedom would be granted soon. She knew that, if it hadn't already occurred, I, too, would soon be forced to submit to the fleshly lusts of one or more of the hired hands or field slaves. So I have remained "the one who waits," the one who waits for life to happen; the one who lets life have its way with me; letting it will itself onto me, instead of being the one willing to make it change by grabbing for what I want most and making it mine.

We were inside the cabin, alone together, making stew in the big pot that hung in the fireplace. I said to Mama emancipation might be more than an idle musing if the South loses the war. But Mama scrawled in the dirt floor with a stick that the defeat of the South wasn't likely to happen. As I stirred the pot, I kept thinking about the President's decree, then whispered to Mama that we might be freed if we could find a way North. I suggested we might stow away on one of the blockade runners, but Mama didn't think we could get onboard unnoticed. We'd be caught before the boat even left port. But with the new information we'd been privy to, I quickly replied that we could get onboard if we hid ourselves in one of the tobacco barrels. We posed possibilities back and forth to each other and wove together plausible plans with credible outcomes until finally Mama agreed we had one that might really succeed.

Mama grew pensive as if, for a while, she was having a silent conversation with herself. Her head tilted down as she methodically cut fresh carrots into bite-sized chunks and tossed them into the black pot. She turned her face to one side then to the other, like there were two opposing forces busy at war within her head until finally, after a time, one of them won out and she came to some resolve. We would sneak into Mr. Pettigrew's storehouse and each hide out in one of the tobacco casks destined for Boston. We'd make the trip as cargo. Five days in a barrel was a small price to pay for what would lay ahead, she wrote. Not a foolproof plan, she said, but bravery is a choice, one made not without fear, but in spite of it. She also wrote, true love

56

meant opening the way for the ones you love and emphasized how much she wanted me to have a chance for freedom. She underlined the word "freedom" with a stick and scraped it back and forth under the word until it wore a deep gully in the sand floor. And she added, "And when you do find it, you've got to hold onto it with all you've got. It is very, very dear." She quickly erased all traces of what she had written in the dirt.

We went about our usual routines for the next few days. I tried hard not to show my excitement about our planned adventure. Even though this plantation is the only home I'd ever known, I felt no attachment to it. As long as Mama and I would be traveling together, that was all that mattered.

Friday night, just before sunset, we slipped quietly away from the plantation and hurried through the forest of tall oaks in the direction of the Pettigrew plantation. We neared the edge of the small pasture that led to the farmyard. Silhouetted against the purple sky were Mr. Pettigrew's large storage barns. A thin horse stood patiently in front of the cavernous doorway of the first storehouse while a few men loaded burlap-shrouded bales of cotton onto the wagon that was hitched behind the horse. Around the far side, at the rear of the building, two more horse-and-wagon teams stood tied and unattended. These wagons were already loaded, one piled high with the big blocks of tightly bound cotton and the other with oaken barrels. Even from a distance we caught the heavy sweet scent of the cured tobacco coming from the kegs.

We watched as the last trace of the sun had dipped below the horizon. The rising new moon offered little light to give us away. Mama held out an oil-cloth pouch that contained my parchment diary, a small wooden cross Mama's brother, Henry had carved for her long ago, Uncle Henry's old clay pipe, an ivory button, and a small green snuff bottle I salvaged from the master's house and filled with fresh water. These were our most treasured possessions and all that we owned. She motioned for me to put it under my shirt for safe keeping, then waved her hand signaling me to follow behind her. Without a sound, we moved through the darkness and made our way along the edge of the meadow until we were behind the barn. I pointed to one of the wagons then slid silently over its side rail. I deftly pulled up the lids on the barrels one at a time until I found two that weren't fully packed. Carefully, I eased inside one and pushed down hard on the dried leaves and made a comfortable and sizable hollow in the center. I looked at Mama and pointed to the other hogshead then pulled the lid closed over my head and sank down onto the soft pulpy bed at the bottom. Mama pushed down hard on the wooden lid covering my barrel to make sure it was secure then I heard her move toward the other barrel. Though I knew I was safely hidden by the time I heard the men exiting the barn, I was terrified that somehow I'd be noticed. As the driver climbed up onto the wagon seat, I started praying. For a long while my own fear deafened me to all sounds except that of my own heartbeat pounding in my ears.

Chapter Eight

Only be thou strong and very courageous, that thou mayest observe to do according to all the law, which Moses My servant commanded thee: turn not from it to the right hand or to the left, that thou mayest prosper whithersoever thou goest. (Joshua 1:7)

The long, rutted and bumpy road rocked and jostled me against the sides of my small, cramped space. I braced myself snugly against the wooden staves, and soon the tobacco compressed down from the swaying of the wagon and gave me more room inside the barrel. After a short while the wagon came to a halt.

Sounds of heavy boots crunching gravel grew louder as someone approached and spoke to the driver.

"Follow this road north until it forks. The right fork will take you to the harbor. You'll find *The Bald Eagle* tied up at the first pier. There'll be someone to help you unload your cargo onto her deck. It's dark with a heavy fog over the water so you shouldn't be noticed, but try to be quick," the man said.

"I will." answered the driver. He clucked to the horses and the wagon began to move again.

The fresh, cool air that had wafted into the barrel smelled pleasantly of the salty sea. Now the wagon creaked gently as it rolled over softer ground, then the big, heavy wheels slowed and rolled to a stop.

Unseen hands slid the kegs along the floorboards and the cart was repeatedly rocked forward and back. One after another they were unloaded, each making a dull thud on the loose sand. Then someone tugged at my barrel and pulled it roughly across the wood. With a bump I was dropped down and slid again. Nearby, an engine hissed and gurgled. I could feel its rumble beneath my feet.

"Cast off the lines," someone said. "Let's get this bucket of bolts underway. Remember stoke 'er only with hard coal 'til we get to the open sea."

"Aye, Aye, Cap'n," another voice answered.

"And if you run out, start fuelin' 'er with some of that cotton soaked in turpentine. It'll give us more speed and won't make no smoke trail to give us away."

"Yes sir, Cap'n, sir," another man answered smartly. "We'll keep her fired up good and strong 'til we rendezvous with the *Peregrine*."

The chug-chug of the engine quickened its pace. We were moving.

From the little I could see through the cracks and knotholes in the hogshead, I was now on the blockade running steamer. All night the engine roared under the deck - it was probably cranked to near full power. At the first light of dawn there were shouts that the *Peregrine* was spotted awaiting our arrival, and men began moving around the deck of the steamer to prepare to tie up alongside her. Thick ropes and pulleys were secured and the bales of cotton and casks of tobacco and turpentine were hoisted aboard the big ship. My barrel and the other hogsheads were lashed to her gunwales, and the cotton was taken and stored below-decks.

Once a-sea, the motion of the boat to lulled me to sleep. The ship moved smoothly and silently save for the sound of the rigging singing in the breeze and the canvas sails billowing with the respirations of the wind. For how long I slept, I do not know. It may have been only a few hours or it could have been an entire day, but when I awoke, rays of saffron sunlight were flowing into the barrel through the spaces in the wood staves. I peeked out through one of the cracks and saw the sky, blue as a robin's egg, and the sea, like liquid mercury, glinted in the sun. When I tired of peering out at my surroundings I took my diary book from under my clothes and unwrapped it carefully to not break the pencil that was tucked into a little pocket of the its leather covering. I wanted to keep track of the days. I opened the book and started to read the last entry - words written in Mama's own hand. My blood went cold.

My Dear Celia,

I love you more than words could ever express. You are my one and only joy, so please understand my reasons for what I have done. I did not stow away in the wagon nor on the ship and will not be with you when you arrive in the North. In Boston I would be far more a hindrance to you than a help. With your beautiful light skin and God-given loveliness you will be welcomed and easily accepted by the people who live where you are going. Alone, there will be many more possibilities open to you than if I was with you. My deformities would only bring shame upon you and prevent you from achieving all that I wish for you. I have always prayed that you would know days more wonderful than any you've known before. God has answered my prayers by showing me a way to give you the best chance for a free life and a better future filled with happiness and opportunity - a chance to walk out of the shadows and into the light.

We are like two trees growing from the same trunk. Sometimes they must bend away from each other to reach for the sun. Sometimes one tree breaks and falls, but the remnant of stump will always be there as a support so the other one can keep standing and grow strong, tall and mighty. I want to help you, Celia, to spread and grow into a beautiful, mag-

61

nificent tree. That's what a mother's love is for. That's what a mother wants to do - make a way for her child to flourish.

Don't be sad for me. I am not returning to Shamrock Valley. For now, I hope to get above the Union lines and plan to make a place for myself to wait out the war - alone in the wilderness. That is where I am most at home. Please stay brave, my baby girl - and always aware of God's angels around you. Remember the scripture, "He will command his angels concerning you to guard you in all your ways." Through them He will show you the way through the days and weeks ahead, and in time, will show us both the way back to each other.

My love is with you forever,

Mama.

Before I had gotten even half-way through the letter, tears poured down my face onto the page, and I finished reading it through blurry eyes. Sadness and panic seized me and overtook reason. Even if it meant returning to the plantation, I wanted to be back with Mama. But logically, I knew that was impossible and unwise, and risking discovery now would be foolish and dangerous. A reluctant traveler, with no escape from my anguish, I had embarked on a course I was now unable to alter. I bore my misery in silence, but my heart cried out for an unknown location: - somewhere in Virginia, on the patch of ground where Mama stood.

Chapter Nine

*For Thou hast been a strength to the poor, a strength to the
needy in his distress, a refuge from the storm, a shadow from the
heat, when the blast of the terrible ones is as a storm against the
wall. (Isaiah 25:4)*

The movement of the ship was different now, - its pitching and rolling more forceful and menacing. To keep my precious belongings
safe, I knotted my pouch closed and bound it around my waist with
its lacings. Sea spray and rain fiercely pelted the lid above me. A
cold, chill wind whistled across the tiny spaces between the slats,
and small droplets of water traced their way down and searched for
an entrance through the cracks. The ropes, creaked and groaned and
loosened with every swell. My barrel threatened to shift. In another
part of the ship I could hear a deck hand scream we were headed
into a nor'easter, and others were yelling for more crew to tighten
down slack lines. No one noticed my barrel slipping or that it was no
longer secured. It skidded again and again, first one way across the
wet deck and then back again. The distance increased the each time.
It collided with other objects that had also broken free. Suddenly,
in the blink of an eye, the barrel hit hard against something and
gave me a terrible jolt. I was thrown against the side of the barrel,
and then I was falling, rolling, spinning - the keg, with me inside,
tumbled overboard and crashed into the now-angry, perilous sea.

The staves cracked from the impact. Though the hogshead held together, it was rapidly filling with seawater. I was trapped and sinking. What had been my refuge would soon be my coffin. Desperately, I pushed up on the lid, but it didn't budge. I kicked hard with both feet, over and over again, until it finally gave way. The water rushed into the storm-tossed barrel as it continued to sink lower and lower beneath the surface. I rose up through the opening and swam hard. Desperate for air I struggled. Coughing and choking, I treaded water to stay afloat, and kept myself from being swallowed up by the turbulent ocean that tried to drown me.

As I rose and fell on the huge ocean swells, I heard nothing but the howling wind in my ears. Sea and sky were an iron-gray void. It was impossible to tell where one ended and the other began. Here, the brawny God of the North Wind had coupled with the monstrous Ruler of the East Wind. Both, with bloated cheeks puffed out wide, blew with supernatural force. Thunder rumbled like boulders rolling in the heavens. I was adrift in the domain of giants, the creators of violent rainstorms, gales and tempests, who live here and reign supreme. Their violent tempers had conjoined and their furies merged to be unleashed upon the elements in a union of relentless force.

I strained my eyes to see through the leaden mist. In the torrent, a shape took form. A floating cask, with other pieces of flotsam, was drifting directly towards me, lifted high on the the crests of the waves then dropping low into the troughs. They were pushed closer by each great, heaving breath blown forth by the gale. Finally the barrel washed within reach, - like a life ring; my only salvation. In the murky darkness I grabbed on and clung to it with both of my exhausted arms.

Time held no meaning. The darkness defined no space. All through the night I clung tightly to the rim of the keg with heavy arms that ached from fatigue and clenched fingers, numb from strain. Swept by the whirlwind, hard rain and sea spray whipped and stung me. Like the long wisps of a wild horse's mane, they lashed my face. The wind, a monstrous beast of Herculean power, forced itself upon me and pushed me beneath each towering mountain of sea in hopes I would succumb to its dominance.

The tempest fought savagely to be victor. Many times I nearly surrendered to it as my master to so end the fight to escape its clutches, and embrace the peace and rest beneath the depths of the sea. Often throughout the long night I slipped into a half-sleep with my head a-bob, barely above the surface. But each time something would nudge my legs dangling like a rag doll's. I was roused from my nightmarish stupor to the briny taste of seawater that streamed down my face and mixed with the salty tears of hopelessness that spilled from my eyes.

In my dazed, semi-conscious state, I dreamt of my mother. We had endured so much anguish, only to be lost to each other now. Visions of her smiling, sweet face formed out of the mist that swirled in the blackness.

She called my name, "Celia, Celia."

"Mama, I'm here," I mumbled. "Over here," but she kept calling.

I was running, running. Gone from my mind was the sea, the wind, the water. I reached out for her, a glowing light in the blackness of night. *Mama, you are my peace and my rest and now you must be my strength.*

"You told me to never give up, Mama. No, I won't give in. I will try…, I will try to hold on…, and survive," I gasped. "We will find each other again!"

Scared and alone with no one to rescue me, I was probably going to die, but I was determined to fight hard until not an ounce of strength remained.

I was awakened by a very subtle push against my foot.

Darkness melted into breaking dawn. The hellish squall had passed. I had prevailed, and the rising, bright yellow sun revived my faith. Yes, in my heart and in my soul, there was hope. The sea had flattened and was once again quiet, tranquil and tame. Its syrupy surface, showing barely a ripple, felt soft and thick against my skin. My eyes burned from the salt. My vision was blurry, but faintly, I could see a ghostly shape rising from the depths. The foggy form grew clearer and larger as it ascended through the calm, green water. Huge and light gray, it surfaced like a locomotive puffing out steam, and it spouted a fountain of water up into the cool morning air. Higher it rose. Lifting its colossal ivory head, it slowly turned and glided directly toward me. I gasped. Defenseless and terrified, for a long time I forgot to exhale. Amazingly, the demeanor of this magical creature was not malicious or fierce. Instead, it somehow seemed gentle. It passed beside me. Its massive dark, but kindly eye, fixed on me with a look of curiosity. Was this real, I asked myself? Or am I delirious?

Without effort, the white whale submerged and reappeared again. Now very near, it rolled on its side to get a better view of me. Its huge eye conveyed an ancient wisdom. It searched my face and locked its gaze with mine as if trying to see into my soul. I reached out my hand as it passed and lightly touched its body, pale as the clouds and as smooth as the finest silk charmeuse. I knew the familiar feel of that silken skin, I thought. Had this leviathan been with me through the night?

I spoke to it, and it seemed to be listening. "Did you push the floating barrels my way? Was it you who kept jostling me awake? I believe it was! You wanted to save me from death… I owe you many thanks," I said to the beautiful, sleek animal.

The whale, nearly motionless, watched me very closely as I continued.

"Are you white because you're old?" I mused. "Or maybe that's just the color of your skin." Very slowly, it glided past again and moved its almond-shaped eye to keep me in its view. Again it blew air and a spray of water up towards the sky.

"Are you wondering what I am? Or maybe you've done this all before…" Again it blew air and a spray of water upwards.

"Or do you look hard at me because I'm so dark,… and you're so white?" I quipped.

It circled back a few more times and continued its investigation of me, then swam off - but not too far away. It stayed nearby through-out most of the day, then later in the afternoon, it gave a flip of its broad tail as if waving good-bye, and was gone.

Chapter Ten

Remember ye not the former things, neither consider the things of old. Behold, I will do a new thing; now it shall spring forth; shall ye not know it? I will even make a way in the wilderness, and rivers in the desert. (Isaiah 43: 18-19)

Each time I scanned the horizon it was unchanged, except this time. I counted the small dark shape just above the level line of the ocean as a mirage or just a trick of the sun, but as time passed, it grew larger. After a couple of hours I recognized it as a large sailing ship. It was moving very slowly and strangely. Though it had three masts and many sails, it also had plumes of dark smoke streaming out from its center, almost as if it was burning. The ship headed toward me, and I could do nothing to move out of its path. Closer and closer it came; so close that I could clearly make out three men standing at the ship's railing, near the most forward mast. One was pointing while he looked through a spyglass. Other men had lowered a small boat over the side. It was manned by two men. One was rowing, and the other was pointing in my direction. I hid behind the barrel, but it was useless to try to conceal myself.

"There. Over, there," said the man pointing.

"Aye, Cap'n!" said the man at the oars.

"Ahoy, there. Can you hear me?" the first man called, speaking through a horn that made his voice a great deal louder than that of the other man.

I looked closely at the boat and then at the men. I feared the strangers, but also knew I wouldn't survive much longer afloat on the sea.

"Can you understand me? We can help you." the man called through the horn. "If you stay out here, you'll surely die."

I moved to the other side of the cask to get a clearer view of their faces. Their speech was unusual. I understood their words, but the men didn't speak like anyone I had heard back home.

"I'll throw a kisbee to you. Grab onto it, and we'll pull you in."

The man stuck the horn in his belt and cast me a large brown ring with a rope attached. Outlined against the sun, the captain stood in the small boat. He was a burly and robust man, hearty and strong. Not tall, but impressive of stature. He tossed the ring easily and with such accuracy that it landed right beside me and floated on the glass-flat water. I held it with one arm, and it bore all my weight without sinking.

"Go ahead, now. Put it over your head, and hold on to it."

I did as he said. He pulled the rope, hand over hand, until I was at the side of the small rowboat.

"Now, take my arm. We'll help you over the gun'l," instructed the captain matter-of-factly.

"Sakes alive, Cap'n, it's a girl! And a negro girl at that!" said the other man as he helped heft me over the side.

I sat shivering as both men stared at me in disbelief. Seawater dripped from my tattered dress. It ran down my bare legs and puddled around my feet. Quickly I hid my pouch, still secured around my waist, safely in the folds of my wet dress.

"Campbell, put that Guernsey coat about her before she gets chilled," ordered the Captain.

"And take this blanket to cover yourself in," he said to me, "until we can get you some other clothes from the slop chest onboard the ship." He offered me a dark wool blanket that I quickly took and wrapped around every part of me that wasn't covered by the woolen coat.

"Man the oars, Campbell," the captain said as he filled a ladle partway from a spigot on a small wooden keg. He held out the ladle with very large, strong hands.

Looking toward the ship, he said, "Take a couple of small sips. No more or it will make you sick." The captain was brusque but his way was kind.

I had barely enough strength to raise the dipper, but the water soothed my cracked lips and dry, parched mouth. I craved more, but heeded the captain's warning.

We neared the ship. Most of the gray smoke had dissipated, and through bleary eyes, I could see it had come from a raised, bricked box behind the center mast. Just a few thin puffs of white smoke floated up from the two black smokestacks protruding from it. The deck was a flurry of activity - with men lowering casks down into the hold. Others were scrubbing the deck, and still more were splashing it with buckets of seawater and flushing it clean.

Two of the crew tugged on rope pulleys and raised us up to the deck. When the little boat was secured, the captain stood over me, and lifted me in his arms as if I was a mere doll. I was too weak to protest. He was a stout and rugged man, but he carried me with surprising gentleness as he climbed over the rail and made his way toward the stern of the ship. With me still limply draped across his arms, he stepped nimbly down wooden steps and unlatched a door that opened into a spacious cabin. He placed me on a soft bed in a corner alcove. After days of agony, I struggled to stay awake on the delightfully comfortable bed.

"The name's MacGregor - Eben MacGregor. And I'm the captain of this barque. These are my quarters," he gestured with a sweep of his arm, "but you can rest here until you're feeling stronger. I can take the couch in the sitting area so you can have some privacy. You'll be safe in here."

"We can find a shirt and slops for you to wear so you can get out of those wet clothes. I'll tell the cook to bring you a ladle of hot broth - but remember, just a few sips at a time."

"Thank you, sir," I managed to whisper hoarsely. He had the definite air of authority, though I didn't feel him to be at all overbearing.

He asked, looking down at me, "Can you tell me your name, missy?"

I looked up drowsily; my eyelids heavy and sleepy. His roundish face, pleasant, almost jovial, was framed by waves of thick chestnut hair and topped by a near-black, flat-topped captain's hat. He had a full beard, coppery and short. His nose was rather large and broad. He resembled a drawing of a Viking that hung on the wall in the Master's study at Shamrock Valley. But his eyes, I remember his eyes - honest and blue; kind eyes that danced as he spoke.

"Celia," I muttered before dozing off.

I was awakened by a knock on the door. It was Campbell carrying a warm cup of broth, a dry cotton shirt and white canvas trousers.

"Here y'are, missy. Some warm soup and dry clothes for ya'. Ya' best get out of your wet dress 'afore ya' catch a death. I'll leave ya' to it." He left the clothes on a bench and placed the cup of broth in a holder by the bed.

"Thank you, sir." I took a few sips of the warm liquid and quickly changed into the rough shirt and trousers. I tucked my pouch underneath the baggy front of the tunic. I lay back on the bed, unable to hold back the veil of sweet slumber any longer.

Chapter Eleven

*Every good gift and every perfect gift is from above, and cometh
down from the Father of lights, with whom is no variableness,
neither shadow of turning.*
(James 1:17)

I think I slept for two days straight. I awoke to find another tin cup
of broth beside the bed, and a worn, but still good pair of brown brogans on the floor in front of the nightstand. After sipping the soup, I
got out of bed and slipped them on my feet. There wasn't much left
to my old shoes. They were but three pieces of leather, worn through,
and barely held together by the lacings. I held up my old, tattered
dress that was in a heap on the bench. It wasn't much more than
a rag. I looked at these frayed items to decide whether I wanted to
keep them or toss them into the sea. The memories attached to them
were bittersweet. As slave clothes, they were reminders of my bondage, but to me they were also symbols of a time remembered - of the
happiness Mama and I shared. They were what I had been wearing
when we were last together, and I had to keep them. I stuffed the old
things under the bed. My life was changing by inches.

The cabin was sparsely furnished, but very neat and tidy. Three
large windows that opened out lined one wall of the stern gallery,
and though the room was sunny and warm, only one window was
ajar. A vista of clear blue sky and silvery ripples of cobalt water

brightened the space of the open-sash window like a moving panorama. It was lovely. I sat down again on the edge of the bed. I was uneasy about where I was being taken and fearful about where the ship would be putting into port.

Footsteps sounded down the companionway and there came a knock on the closed door. After a moment the captain entered.

"Well," he said. "Welcome aboard! You're looking better! Not as groggy as you were!"

As I took another mouthful I said, "I'm feeling stronger. Thank you for the clothes and the soup."

"Glad to hear it!"

"So,… Where do you hail from, Celia?" He pulled the chair out from his desk and sat facing me. "And how did you come to be adrift in the sea?"

"Well, I was going north, sir, to Boston; onboard a ship…, and I fell overboard in the storm," I was nervous and worried he would surmise I was a runaway. I prepared for the worst.

"Might anyone be looking for you?" he asked.

His strange accent was like listening to an odd type of music; one I'd never heard before. I had to tune my ear to the interesting sounds, otherwise I found myself paying attention to how he spoke instead of to what he was saying.

"Uh, no, not that I know of, sir. I was traveling alone."

"Isn't someone awaiting your arrival?" He pursued the questioning and tried to uncover the original purpose of my voyage.

"Yes, sir. Well, no, …not exactly. I gave them no precise arrival date," I lied. I didn't want to answer his questions. These people, this ship, its destination, …all of it terrified me.

"I see," he said still looking at me thoughtfully. He averted his eyes as if he knew I was not telling the complete truth, but he chose not to pursue it.

"Ok. Well… It'll be a couple of weeks before reaching home port, and you're welcome to stay in my cabin. Can't very well have you bunking in the seaman's quarters," he said - shaking his head and raising an eyebrow.

"Don't worry, you'll find me a gentleman in every way," he added humbly. Noticeably uncomfortable, his cheeks reddened a bit as he quickly turned away and cleared his throat.

"Captain," I ventured. Fearing his answer, I held my breath. "Exactly where is home port?"

"Why, New Bedford, my dear. Our home port is New Bedford," he said. I exhaled in relief. At least the ship would be landing at a port in the North.

"You'll find it a safe harbor." He turned and again glanced at me with one tawny eyebrow raised.

I was sure he suspected I was an escaped slave, and my anxiety and dread overtook me so completely, my hands trembled.

"You can belay that," he said, "You've no need to fret. In case you're wondering, I side with the abolitionists. Always have. In fact, I've got two runaway slaves as hands on the ship. It won't be easy to get started once you get ashore, but there you'll find many people of the same mind as I."

He continued, "As soon as you're up to it, you can earn your keep and help out the cook. He can use the assistance and it'll give you a chance to see the ship. Anyhow, you'd go stir crazy staying shut up in this cabin for the rest of the trip." He smiled. His eyes glinted in the sunlight.

"Thank you, Captain. That's very kind." I looked directly at him and beamed with sincerity.

It seemed his nature to be authoritative and commanding, but there seemed a side of his character that was also well-meaning and considerate.

"Come up on deck, when you're ready, and I'll introduce you to Murphy, our cook." With that he rose and left.

74

New Bedford. I didn't know if I should be relieved or sad. With every hour I was moving farther and farther away from Mama. It was a blessing, though, that my rescuers were Yankees and not Southerners who would be likely to turn me in for the reward money offered for any escaped slave. I was sure the captain guessed I was running to freedom, but his directness in revealing where his sympathies lay gave me some assurance of safety, at least until reaching port. He certainly seemed to be frank and straightforward and with a certain spark of charisma thrown in. I had two weeks to figure out if his abolitionist beliefs ran down to the pith and marrow of his bones, and to decide whether I could trust that he will allow me to go free once we reached land. I must be ready with a plan to sneak ashore alone if, in the days ahead, he gave me reason to doubt his honesty.

The captain introduced me to the cook and left us to get acquainted. I helped Murphy light a fire in the big cast iron stove that nearly filled the small space of the topside galley. The stove was bolted to the deck for safety. It had rails around the top to keep the pots and pans from sliding and tipping in rough seas. Below deck was a larger area that served as a kitchen pantry and dining area where the crew was fed in shifts. Murphy informed me that the first round of diners would be the captain and mates, then came the able seamen, next in rank. The ordinary seamen ate meals less elegant, and the food was brought up to them on deck. The cook was quite pleasant even though, on the outside, he looked crusty and crotchety. Within a day we were good workmates and enjoyed each other's company, too.

We were readying the pots of food to be brought up for cooking one morning and I asked,

"Murphy, how long have you been doing the cooking onboard."

"Oh, going on over ten years now, I been with Cap'n MacGregor on the *Lady Grey*, and I'll stay on as long as he'll have me. The cap'n 's a good and honest man - copper-bottomed as they come. Never has no problems finding seamen to sign on with 'im. Never lost a ship, neither."

Murphy's words bespoke his great respect for the captain.

"Bout six years ago when the tail end of our voyage took us well to the north, the *Lady* got damaged bad by the ice. But the cap'n, he bound up her hull with chains and got us back to home port, safe and sound. Ever since, they've called us the *Lady in Chains* whenever we came into port!" He chuckled.

"How clever, though! And it worked to get you all back safely! No wonder he's never wanting for sailors!"

"Kinda man who'll get you through anything. Saved my neck many a time. He's a jolly sort, too, mostly - a true gentleman. 'E'll overlook a bit of minor vice, although I don't know that he 'as any himself,…but 'e'll let you to 'ave your own. He don't tolerate no she-nanigans or skulduggery on his ship, though. But you be fair with 'im and you'll never see a heart as big or as generous as the cap'n's," he went on. "You ask anyone aboard, they tell you the same."

He was open and guileless as he went on about the captain.

"If there's one thing abou' the sea, it'll let you know the men that can be counted on and the one's that can't. The cap'n's one who can. Most o' this crew'd follow him into hell if he asked them to."

After a time, Murphy said, "I think we're done here. Let's get this stuff cookin'."

We lugged the two big iron pots up to the galley. One pot held about enough fish chowder to feed twenty men, the other was filled with a stew of salted meat and potatoes. The big iron pots fit tightly on the hot stove top. We went back for the biscuits and duff and put them into the belly of the black stove. Murphy told me our work was complete, and he wouldn't need me again until late morning.

In just the short time I had been aboard, I observed that the captain commanded the crew with the firm hand of an absolute ruler. As a taskmaster, he demanded obedience, but always with regard

76

for the dignity and self-esteem of his men. Regardless of rank, he awarded each the respect that was due him. As I plainly saw, the men returned his fair leadership with great admiration, loyalty and honor, and they took pride in their work.

Some afternoons from an out-of-the-way spot on the mid-deck, I enjoyed the sea air and watched as, lithe and limber as squirrels, seamen ran up the ratlines to adjust sails and sheets aloft at such great heights that from the deck, they looked the size of small birds. They sang sea chanties, side by side. They sang out as they tied off ropes, made fast the sails, and climbed through the rigging in rhythm to their chanting. Their refrains eased their labor. Their movements were buoyant, almost cheerful. Their voices rang throughout the ship much like the slaves' songs carried through the fields back home. Most of the seamen were white. Some were Negro. A few others were from unknown places far away. They toiled together on the ship and helped each other with no notice of color nor prejudice toward race.

All were friendly and amiable to each other and to me, except for one of the foremast hands who was called Walker. While he worked, he would cock his head to the side, like a raven, saucy and bold. He taunted his workmates then leered at them with one beady eye at a time, as he tried to goad one of them into a scuffle. With no takers, he sauntered across the deck to ascend another Jacob's ladder. He repeated the same tactic until, finally, he was admonished by the mate to pipe down or he would be made to run the gauntlet for a flogging by his fellow shipmates. The threat of that seemed to quiet him. I always kept my distance from him and tried to avoid being the object of his unnerving sneer.

One morning, after breakfast, I went back to the cabin to write in my journal and left the door ajar to clear out the stale, musty air. Busily engaged in scrawling my thoughts on the page, I jumped when the door was suddenly pushed open, and Walker strode in.

"What have we here," he said mockingly as he picked up my diary roughly by its cover. "A nigga who can read and write!"

"You must think you're something special… at least the captain seems to think so!" He spat out his vulgar sarcasm with cackling contempt.

He waved my book in the air. "Keepin' you here in this first-rate cabin."

"Please. Give that back to me," I begged.

He towered over me and stared at me with hatred, "He got his own little nigga wench."

I cowered under the mean sting of his hostile and derogatory words, then heard footfalls behind me. Walker quickly put the book down on the table.

A booming bellow from the captain filled the small space with the force of an iron fist.

"Walker! Enough! You've just earned yourself a bread and water ration for three days. Do you care to try for something more?"

"Er, no, sir, captain," he stammered.

"Now get out," the Captain said with the sharpness of a knife's edge. "And from now on you best give Miss Green a wide berth. If you're caught at this end of the ship again, you'll be flogged - or worse."

"Aye, aye, sir, captain, sir." Walker fled.

Chapter Twelve

For I know the plans I have for you," declares the LORD, "plans to prosper you and not to harm you, plans to give you hope and a future. (Jeremiah 29:11)

The spell of fair weather continued, and again, for the fifth day, the water was calm and its movements slow and unhurried. An occasional light breeze made cat's paws that swirled quickly on the surface, and vanished just as fast atop the otherwise thick and syrupy sea.

The mix of wind, water and sky was an intoxicating potion that was captivating and difficult to resist. Whenever I wasn't helping Murphy, I spent a lot of my time up on deck. Always present, like my own breath, was the sound of the blue-violet sea, that whished along the sides of the great wooden ship like liquid silk as, heeled over with the wind on her quarter, the *Lady Grey* softly cut her path to the north. High overhead, the fluttering sails gently altered their shapes from momentary shifts of the temperate July wind.

Even at night, when the sky and sea met in a backdrop of deepest blue, the view was a spectacle of natural beauty. Cast from above, silver moonbeams lighted our path and flashed white in the wash of our wake. Multitudes of stars, sprinkled like diamonds in the sky, shimmered their celestial brilliance and, everywhere the phosphorescent sea sparkled a ghostly, spectral green. As I stood on the deck the fresh air filled my nostrils and the mild wind softly caressed my face. *This voyage is an incredible adventure in many ways*, I thought. Far different than the first portion of my sea-faring journey, when I was cramped and hidden away in a barrel.

For a short time each morning and evening, the captain walked the starboard stretch of the sternmost upper deck that was his private retreat. Most of his time, though, was spent on the quarterdeck, just behind the main mast of the ship. That was his domain, his throne, where he reigned supreme. There, he knew the real meaning of freedom that most landsmen can only imagine. Day after day, he showed himself to be a most benevolent ruler. A man of principles, he took seriously his responsibility for the safety and success of his crew and ship. Yet, he accomplished it all with exacting ease and an economy of means.

"Good morning, Celia," said the captain as he walked toward me from the quarterdeck. "I see you enjoy being in the open air."

"I do, very much, captain. You're so at home here on the ocean, but to me it is all so strange, and new. So beautiful!"

"Yes, it can be quite exhilarating, but sometimes I think if I had any sense, I'd stay ashore!" he said with a chuckle.

"I suppose you must get lonely for your family," I replied.

"Haven't much of a family. My wife passed on five years ago. We never had any children. I just have a sister, who lives in Boston with her husband and four children. Do you have family in New Bedford?"

"The only family I have is my mama. She's still down South. I fear for her with the war still all around her. She refused to make the trip, but insisted I go North. I hope to send for her soon," I answered.

"That'd be wise. I don't think the South can hold out much longer, from what I hear. Things'll get pretty bad in most parts of the Confederacy, if they haven't already," he continued as we both gazed out over the sea.

"What's New Bedford like?" I turned to look at him.

"Well, it's a bustling seaport, fishing and whaling, and lots of merchant ships with cargo coming in and going out - whale oil, cotton goods, cordage... and it's a port of call for a slew of steamers. There's a big business district and industrial center. It's one of the richest cities in the North," he said with enthusiasm.

"It sounds exciting, and teeming with activity," I commented.

"I can assure you, it's a lively place."

He went on to tell me all about the New Bedford area starting with the busy mills that manufactured varied products. He told me hundreds of farms, large and small, dotted the landscape beyond the city, and there were acres of soggy, russet-tinged cranberry bogs and neatly rowed fields of blueberry orchards. Nearby colleges and schools were some of the world's best, and the general population had a such a penchant for culture that the region had grown into a major gathering place for artists, writers and scholars.

"Runaway slaves like Ben, your cabin boy, and the ship blacksmith, Shadrach,... were they proclaimed free when they reached New Bedford? " I inquired.

"Sure. They were considered free men as soon as they set foot on Massachusetts soil. Shadrach got to New Bedford only a few months afore we sailed. Ashore, he had a bad case of the collywobbles and kept pretty much to himself. Whenever he was about town, he was always looking over his shoulder. He was nervous he might be recognized and caught. But, New Bedford's probably the safest and friendliest place there is for an escaped slave."

"It's against the law to buy or sell a slave there, and even if some muckety-muck slave master tracked one of their slaves to Massachusetts, it'd be highly unlikely the abolitionists would allow him to steal back the runaway. Abolitionists can quickly sweep fugitive slaves into hiding, or secretly get them to safety elsewhere in a hurry, until the threat of recapture has passed. And they have the means to filibuster the courts long enough 'til the Confederate skilamalink gives up and goes home with his tail down.

"Who are those you call the abolitionists?" I asked.

"I'd say more than two thirds of the people of New Bedford are against slavery. Many of the most avid abolitionists are Negroes. Frederick Douglass, for one, an escaped slave himself, made it to New Bedford and lived there until not long ago. Thomas Dalton, a free Negro, has fought hard for the education of Negroes in white communities of Boston,… but many more are white. They've all helped to organize and mobilize very dedicated groups that will take quick action to keep any Negro from being put back to slavery. They're very vigilant, and together, have extensive resources."

"Celia, is something causing you worry?" He paused then went on. "From years at sea I might seem kind of rough around the edges, but I'm a God-fearing man and I believe the Bible passage that reads: 'every man should eat and drink and enjoy the good of all his labor.' That is one of the gifts of God above, and everyone deserves the right to life, liberty and the pursuit of their own happiness.

"Many times, I have seen the faces of slaves who had just arrived in New Bedford and been privy to some of their grim stories. In no way can I fathom that it is right for one man to own another. Not everyone, though, even in the North, stands on that side of the issue, and I would guess for a Negro, even one as light-skinned as you, that can be troubling. Whatever your concerns, Celia, tell me. I'd be glad to do whatever I can to help."

I gazed down into the water, not yet wanting to divulge my secret openly. There was a risk of betrayal or deception by any one of the crew knowing a fugitive slave bounty could be collected for turning me in. If I was certain I could completely trust the captain, 'fessing up to him about my status might prove best, as he would be able to warn me of the many unforeseen dangers that lurked in this big, mysterious and unfamiliar city that I was about to enter. But, to every thing there is a season, and a time to every purpose under heaven. We were still many days from port, and I had sufficient time to decide my right course of action.

"Thank you, Captain, but I was just curious,… about the way Northerners feel towards Negroes."

"There are places Negroes have made their own,…. But, yes, there are some places Negroes still aren't welcome," he answered with less fervor.

Perhaps because these few days passed so uneventfully, and there was little else to do, the captain spared time each morning to stop and chat with me on deck. I looked forward to our conversations and I think he enjoyed them, as well. Each afternoon when he went into his cabin to the nook lined with rolls of nautical charts, he would summon me. While we bent over the large map spread out on the map table, he traced our plotted route and pointed out our present location. He was surprised to learn I was able to read and write and showed me a shelf of books he kept in a cabinet by the window. I marveled at his books - some on navigation and science, a book by Charles Dickens, another about travel to the China Sea, the Holy Bible, and many others I longed to browse. He pulled out a leather-bound book by Henry Wadsworth Longfellow, one of his best-loved, and one he thought I might like. He handed it to me. He said Longfellow, also an anti-slavery supporter, lived not too far from New Bedford, and his poetry had become extremely popular - not only in America but in Europe as well. I grasped the book eagerly. Noting my keen interest as I browsed the pages of poems, he offered me use of the little library anytime I fancied. That brought a beaming smile of appreciation to my face, and a sunny bit of mirth to his.

Chapter Thirteen

God saw all that He had made, and it was very good. And there was evening, and there was morning--the sixth day. (Genesis 1:31)

I went to the galley to start the chores with Murphy. I offered to do the cooking for the day. He led me down to the storeroom below deck. Each of us carried a basket to tote the needed ingredients to the steward's cabin where we prepared the meal for cooking in the galley stove, above. My basket included a fresh-killed duck and potatoes, for the main course, and saved from their last stop in the tropics, some dried pineapple and papaya for me to bake into a pie. Murphy's basket contained salt horse, the less savory dried meat staple of the ordinary seamen, flour, and lard along with some hard bread, dried beans and molasses.

While I seasoned the duck and cut potatoes, Murphy told me he and his wife were immigrants from Ireland and had landed in Boston in spring of 1853. He ended up in New Bedford soon after arriving, to seek work on a fishing boat. He heard the *Lady Grey* was in need of a cook and she was ready to depart as soon as one was secured. The captain didn't even ask him if he knew how to cook. He hired him on the spot, saying "I like the cut of your jib. Sign on and we sail tomorrow at dawn." Murphy said it was the best thing that ever happened to him. Even though he was only a fair cook, he improved with practice and the captain has kept him on for every voyage since. After the captain's wife died, he employed Murphy's wife, Ellen, to housekeep for him twice a month while he's at sea.

"Losing his wife must have grieved him," I said while I mixed the filling for the pie.

"Like nothin' I'd 'er 'afore seen," Murphy answered. "She died of the influenza while we were a'sea. I was wi' him when we rowed ashore an' 'e opened the letter that awaited 'im. He wept like a man crazed. Weren't sure he was goin' ta come out o'it. 'E rowed himself back to th' ship and n'e'er came ashore for three years. Wonderful woman she was, too. Jennie was 'er name. Th' apple o' his eye. The cap'n keeps 'er picture on 'is bed stand 'n 'is cabin."

"Yes, I saw the photograph there. I assumed it was his wife. She was very beautiful."

"T'is a cryin' shame she die' so young," he answered.

I heard in Murphy's voice the empathy he felt for the captain and with his words I glimpsed the man the captain was, and better understood the man I saw now.

Murphy brought the bean pot up to the stove. When he returned he dipped a finger into the bowl of filling I had concocted.

"Mmm,mmm! The cap'n 's goin' to fire me if you keep makin' him special treats like this pie," he teased.

"I'm grateful to him. He's been very hospitable AND he saved my life,… The least I can do for him is cook some of his favorite foods," I said and grinned as I wiped my hands on a dishrag.

"Yea," Murphy said, "cause one thing about the cap'n, he loves t' eat!" He roared at his own humor until he was bent in two and got me chuckling, as well.

When he recovered from his fit of laughter he said, "I almost forgot! Since you're makin' such a fancy pie for the cap'n's table, there's a pie crimper in the cupboard. It'll make pretty edges on th' crust."

Murphy climbed topside to put the duck into the oven. I opened the cabinet, and on a hook was an intricately carved cutting wheel with a exquisitely formed handle in the shape of a mermaid. I trimmed the pie and brought it up to the galley stove to bake.

I rang the dinner bell in the galley and carried the pie down to the pantry cupboard. Murphy brought the other pots of food down to the table. The captain and mates, impatient and famished, took their places at the table and filled their plates with food. The meat disappeared quickest - even the drippings were sopped up with the soft biscuits until the pot was clean.

"Now here's somethin' special - just for the cap'n. Celia baked a fine lookin' pie for dessert," announced Murphy.

He sliced the warm pie and passed it around, first to the captain then to the others. From 'round the table came exclamations of praise as the first sweet forkfuls were enjoyed.

"Delectable, Celia!" said the captain. He savored each bite.

"Finest pie we et so far this voyage," the first mate joked and taunted the cook with his elbow. The rest of the crew sounded off in agreement.

"I gotta agree with that, and she even put fancy edges on the crust!" Murphy complimented.

"That's such a beautiful pie wheel, Murphy" I said. "Is it yours?"

"Emilio, the carpenter, give it to me last Christmas. He carved it outta whalebone. Did a fine job," he answered.

"It must have taken hours of work!" I said. "But where would he get whalebone?"

"The *Lady*'s a whale ship. We been out a'sea huntin' whales for nigh on a year an' some months…., for their oil and baleen bone" said the captain as we filed out of the dining pantry for the next round of crew members to take their dinner.

"But it is such a wondrous beast," I said.

"A beast, indeed, and there is great demand for its oil and baleen. It is rather dirty and gruesome work, I will admit, but because of whale oil New Bedford is known the world over as 'the city that lit the world'! Every factory's machines are lubricated with the oil of the whale's blubber, and there'd be no ladies' corsets or buggy whips without whale baleen," he continued.

"Captain, the night of the storm…, a whale…, saved my life - a ghostly white whale.

The captain and I stepped up on deck. Now alone, he stopped and turned towards me as he listened.

"After I was lost overboard, it wasn't long before I was too tired to swim. I would have drowned if it wasn't for the whale."

I told him how, though he might think me delirious, I believed it was the whale who pushed the floating kegs towards me and kept bumping me awake through the night. I described to him in detail my encounter with the white whale after the storm had ended. I swore that I was fully conscious and not in any way delusional. He made no further comment, nor I to him, before he departed to his quarters.

The captain's friendship had been a comfort and encouragement to me. With each day that passed, I knew clearly, our relationship became dearer to me. From my past, I had learned to be wary and distrustful of white folks. The captain's presence, however, was like a warm cloak in wintertime and gave me a sense of well-being that I had only ever felt with my mother. He was a man more full of life than most - bigger than life, even. His strong, gallant character and genuine goodwill rid me of my fear. He turned my soul into a garden of vitality - fresh and alive; and his easy manner was life-giving sunshine to what had been a dark, withered wasteland within me. I sensed so much warmth and tenderness in his heart. It now surprised me to find such a stony place there.

I wrestled with the morality of killing whales. I didn't want our differences to cause a rift between us, but it bothered me that the captain justified the act by the mere dollar-and-cents value of their parts. I wasn't sure why it troubled me more than slaughtering livestock or hunting deer and other game, except that the consciousness of the whale, its very soul, seemed different - somehow more spiritual and sacred.

Chapter Fourteen

But let him ask in faith, nothing wavering. For he that wavereth is like a wave of the sea driven with the wind and tossed.
(James 1:6)

"Whale, ho. Thar she blows," came a yell from the crow's nest.

"Where blows?" came a response from the mate on the deck.

"Three points off starboard bow, There, there," returned the lookout - pointing.

The captain hurried topside and, searching the sea through his spyglass, located the spouting whale. A crewman was excitedly clanging a big brass bell amidships. Another shouted from the hoops high above, "It's a white whale!"

"By God, well I'll be,... it's a...," muttered the captain half to himself, "...never have I seen.....

He tucked away the spyglass.

"Lower the boats," he snapped as he proceeded toward the first starboard dory. "Walker. With me, now. Celia go below with Murphy."

I was panicked,.... they were going after the white whale.

All five hands and the captain boarded the little boat, and it was ready to be lowered down from the davits.

I raced to the first whaleboat yelling, "Please, Captain, don't kill him. Please, not this one. Let him go," but he didn't hear me for all the commotion as all the boats were filling with seamen.

I leaped over the side as the boat was dropping below the edge of the gunwale and, falling a fair distance, landed in the stern of the boat.

"Please let it go, Captain," I pleaded again.

"I don't abide my orders being ignored. I make my livelihood by bringing in whales, Celia, not by letting them go," the captain answered not wavering in his intent. "You should have stayed with the cook to not be witness to the kill."

Perplexed and frustrated, I sat in the stern trying to think of some way to stop the hunt, but all I could do was watch as the captain steered the narrow boat toward the whale. Walker and the other men pulled hard on the oars and drew us in closer to the enormous white form.

A wild, single-mindedness hung in the air. The harpooner took his place at the bow. With the wooden shaft of the harpoon grasped firmly in both hands, Parker was patiently poised with the iron at the ready as the whale, now aware of our presence, turned toward us and dwarfed our little boat with its massive form.

The whale let out a low-pitched sound, like the deep lowing of a cow. An alien song in a language as old as the sea itself.

"They're just dumb beasts," said Walker with a scowl, "dumb enough to let us row right up beside 'em."

"Just a dumb animal! Just a dumb animal! ...That's what the white boss said to my slave mother, 'she's just a dumb animal', right before he cut her," I screamed back. Walker puffed up as if he were about to strike me, but his eyes quickly shifted to the captain. He settled back down low in his seat, but I was impassioned and continued on without restraint.

"Look into its eye. Captain! Look! Look," I cried. "Is that the eye of a dumb animal?"

91

Awaiting the command to drive his harpoon hard into the whale's flesh, Parker turned. The captain now stood behind the harpooner and stared into the limpid eye of the noble and serene white giant. The creature slowly rose before us and cast its shadow over our motionless whaleboat.

"You'd think different if the vicious, bloody devil was trying to thrash you into the sea and drown ye," another man heckled.

"I'd defend myself, too, if I was fighting for my life. Wouldn't you…, fight to survive?" I screamed into the man's face, and in my outburst my foot banged the floorboards with a loud thump.

The behemoth began to move away. Its speed increased with each arc of its gargantuan ivory-colored body.

"Stay back," the captain commanded and gave the signal to the other two boats that had followed us.

"Mr. Campbell, turn us about and go back to the ship."

"But Captain,…" protested Walker - with two of the others chiming in.

"I said turn us about, and take us home. Now." Unequivocally, he demanded obedience to his will.

That night the summer sun set with a crimson grandeur that turned the sea the color of red wine. The deck was peaceful, and the crew quiet except for a faint, hushed and sweet singing of 'Barbara Allen' coming from somewhere near the bow. The captain appeared from below deck. He stood beside me under the twilit sky and leaned on the taffrail.

Without speaking, he looked out over the sea and asked, "Were you a slave, too, like your mother?"

"Yes," I answered soft and low, almost whispering. "I am a fugitive, and so is my mother."

"I thought you might be, but I figured you'd tell me in your own good time."

"The overseer called her an animal, no better than the cattle or the horses in the fields. She was branded with a red hot iron and her tongue was cut out for teaching me to read and write."

I told him what life was like on the plantation and the reasons Mama stayed behind.

"Now I understand your feelings about the white whale," he said as he looked at me kindly and lowered his gaze.

For some moments there was a weighty silence.

"Are you going to turn me in when we reach New Bedford?"

"Certainly not!" He turned to me. "I'd like to offer you employment, if you're agreeable. I'll be staying ashore for quite a while, and I could use someone to do my cooking and manage my house. You'd be safe there, Celia. I'll see to that."

"That's very generous, Captain," I was relieved. "Yes, surely, I am, …agreeable! That would be quite agreeable!" I looked at him and beamed.

He gave a grunt and a nod of approval. His face brightened, and the corners of his eyes crinkled as he chuckled behind his beard.

The ship pressed on towards New Bedford with all canvas up - at full sail. Close-hauled, we were making good speed. With little work to occupy them, the seamen enjoyed their off-watches settled, like lounging dogs, in small clusters about the ship. Some whittled at trinkets they were sculpting from pieces of whalebone. Others spent their time improvising light-hearted ditties and playing music on home-made instruments they had fashioned out of cast-away scraps of wood. The mood was restful and relaxed, and tempers ran cool aboard the homeward-bound ship.

With much leisure time, the captain spent hours telling me incredible tales of his voyages to exotic places. His lively and dynamic nature that made him a born leader, also made him a riveting storyteller. Though he may have been spinning yarns at times, his accounts were captivating, and my amazement inspired him to elaborate even more about the fantastic creatures and bizarre cultures he had come across in his travels. In the tropics of Asia, he had seen wild monkeys and macaques sunbathing on the beach and swimming in the surf. He told me of the frigid region of the far North that was home to an unusual type of whale with a long spiral spike that grew outward from between its eyes - a unicorn. The Inuit people who hunted these whales for food, lived in huts carved out of ice and covered themselves with thick, furry animal skins to keep warm. He told me of the aurora borealis - like rainbows whirling with lightning in the silent wind of electra; a supernatural spectacle of monumental proportion. He described it as merry dancers being spun across the heavens by the majestic hand of the Almighty. He spoke of other oddities in other distant places that he pointed out on a map. At less than thirty-five years of age, the captain had spent a good part of his life at sea, and had seen so much of the world.

"The things you have seen!" I said. "You have such a fascinating life, Captain!"

"It is that," he said with a sigh. "I've been going to sea since I was a lad. Worked my way from cabin boy to first mate. I've held the job of every man on this ship at one time of my life or another - all except for cook. Never was much good at that!" he said, as he tucked his chin to his chest with a hearty chuckle.

"Are you happy to be getting home for a while…, to more familiar surroundings?"

"While I was married to Jennie,… how I looked forward to coming home to her." He sparked at her mention; became more animated, revived as if taking in a beautiful sunrise.

"But after she was taken by the sickness, for a long time I didn't care if I ever returned to New Bedford. I didn't go ashore for over three years. I preferred being aboard ship, so I could avoid going home to an empty house and facing the sad fact that Jennie would never again be there to welcome me."

Absorbed in his own thoughts, the captain grew pensive again, absorbed in his own thoughts. I noted the way he sagged back into his seat. The sadness, though a memory now and not fresh, still pricked his heart. I plainly saw that beneath this strong, commanding figure of a man dwelt a heart so tender. A heart once filled with such love and devotion, now shamelessly admitting to sorrow.

"I'm sorry, I didn't mean to bring up…,"

"No, no, it's alright. Whether fair weather or foul, I've learned to accept what I can not change." He managed something of a smile. "Eventually, we all must."

"Yes, I suppose we must," I agreed. I reflected on my own situation.

Chapter Fifteen

The Light shines in the darkness and the darkness has not overcome it. (John 1:5)

Late one afternoon the call of "Land, ho," sounded from the crow's nest. The repeated shouts initiated a flurry of activity on deck, and all hands were busy making preparations as the rocky coastline of New Bedford came clearer into view. Towards sundown, the vessel, now with her sails reefed, approached the port. The captain ordered the crew to ease the main sheets. Clouds of gray fog, rolling out over the water like puffs of steam, dampened the air and made it thick and heavy with moisture. We moved slowly, but deftly, now, through the narrow inlet to the harbor with just enough forward motion for the *Lady Grey* to answer her helm. I saw the hazy outlines of many similar vessels anchored a bit closer in, and dozens of ships were tied up, two or three deep, along the wharfs that lined the shore.

"Backwind the main," shouted the captain, and soon the the sails started to luff.

The ship languidly glided to an open portion of water, and the captain gave the order to heave-to, and the *Lady Grey* turned gracefully into the light wind. "Set the anchor" was the next given command. With a clanging and scraping of chains and squeaking of the capstan, the anchor slipped down into the water with barely a splash. The ship pulled back on the massive rope lines to drive the anchor hard in the mud, and the *Lady* serenely came to rest a short distance from the New Bedford waterfront.

I retired below to the cabin, out of the way of the crew as they set a stern anchor then began furling the sails and securing the ship under the supervision of the captain and first mate. It might be a day or two before the casks of whale oil could be unloaded, so the ship would be left at anchor with day and night watches to guard her. Although I was closer to freedom than I had ever been before, I was apprehensive about going ashore.

The *Lady Gray* had become my refuge, and my sanctuary. Life onboard the ship was, in some ways, surreal. It was a self-contained existence, separate from the rest of society; a place where life had a comforting constancy and a simplicity. It had its dangers, but it was a world of expected dangers that were straightforward and honest. As for the sea, I had seen its dangerous face, possibly its worst, and I had seen its best, but the rules were always fair. It did not play favorites. The sea was just itself, pure and elemental - the same for one as for another.

More frightening to me was the new, outside world I was about to enter. It appeared a tangled mire of unknowns and mysteries. I could only guess at what would lie before me. My life was set on a new course. It was a moment I had longed for, but I couldn't stop the fear that had me paralyzed in its clutches and made me uneasy about leaving the ship.

When most of the work had been completed, the captain stepped down the companionway and entered the cabin. He was carrying two empty canvas sacks.

"Are you ready to go ashore?" He spoke with a happy lilt to his voice.

"You can use this bag to gather what you need to take with you." He handed one to me, then he filled the other bag with necessities from his sea chest and cupboard. He glanced at me then stopped

97

and put the bag down on a table. He walked over to face me and put a hand on each of my shoulders.

"Are you scared to leave the ship and go into town?"

I nodded. "People will suspect I'm an escaped slave," I blurted out, "and I'm afraid someone might be sent to force me back to the plantation. What if there's nothing you or anyone else can do to stop them?"

"Celia, the last news I got was that Northern soldiers had advanced far down into the South - all the way to Georgia. Slaves who made it to the Union lines were made legally emancipated, then and there. I do have friends of influence," he looked directly into my eyes, "and I will do everything in my power to see that you remain free. My house is only a short distance from the docks, and I know you'll be safe from harm there."

He spoke with complete truthfulness and candor. "In my time commanding a vessel I've learned that any truly honorable leader worth his salt must be courageous and brave. He must, also, always have concern for the welfare of his men. I've tried to uphold those standards at sea and ashore, as well." He paused.

"Tell me, Celia… do you trust me?"

At that moment, I could almost feel my Mama standing beside me reminding me of her words, "stay aware of God's angels around you." And I also recalled the intensity in her voice when she spoke what is indelibly etched into my mind, …"hold onto freedom with both hands, Celia, and never let it go."

"Yes. …Yes, captain, I think I do!" I said. His reassurance bolstered my courage and I felt my taut face broaden into a near smile.

"OK. Let's go, then." He patted my shoulders in a gesture of encouragement that rid me of all but a shred of my foreboding. He had a way about him, a charming confidence, a vibrance, that always changed things for the better. I hefted my sack and followed the captain up the companionway to the manned whaleboat that was ready to carry us the short distance to shore. The crewmen rowed us away from the *Lady*. I looked back at her. With her sails fastened down, bare masts and shrouds standing tall, the *Lady Grey* looked naked and skeletal - but peaceful, in the safe and sheltered harbor.

Screeching gulls swooped low over our heads and eyed us with scrutinizing curiosity. We landed and walked the length of the pier to the street. Some of the crew trudged directly to the entrance of the crowded and noisy King Phillip Tavern. Others made their way up Water Street, home to the open arms of loved ones long awaiting their return.

Murphy stopped and turned to say goodbye and added in his thick Irish brogue,

"Don't you worry, you'll b' fine here, Celia. I think you'll like it 'n New Bedford." He waved then walked up the street, and followed the others who were headed home.

The captain hailed a hackman who was standing idle at the edge of the square.

"Take us to 380 County Street," the captain said impersonally without looking up at the driver so as to avoid engaging him in conversation. We stepped into the closed-sided carriage. Without a word the driver raised the reins, and the dark horse clip-clopped away from the docks.

Along the quiet street we passed several clapboard rooming houses, many large warehouses of red brick and stone, a crisp, well-kept white shingled establishment named, The Village Inn, and the darkened storefront windows of shops that were closed up for the night. The evening air tasted moist and delicious and was so heavy with mist that the tops of the burning street lamps wore golden halos of light.

After five blocks the carriage stopped. I waited in the shadows behind the wheels while the captain paid the driver his fare. Facing me was a fine, gracious mansard with an ornately-corbeled roof and a projecting bay, like the arc of a rainbow that made the front of the residence resemble the prow of a ship. At the highest point was a crested turret with windows like large spectacles looking to the sea. Altogether, it bespoke opulence, and that the captain was, undoubtedly, a man of means. We passed through a gate at the end of the walk and entered through the front door. Inside, the rooms were elegantly decorated with wonderful furnishings collected from all corners of the globe, and all was kept with a ship-shape tidiness that befitted a sea captain.

"Let's get your things stowed upstairs," he said - indicating the stairway which took us to the second floor.

"You can take this spare room. It should be in good order. While I'm away a charwoman comes weekly to keep the place clean."

The captain continued to another room at the end of hallway and left me to get settled. The room was lovely and had traces of a feminine touch; his wife's, no doubt. The elegantly tasseled drapes were of a cheerful pink-and-green floral chintz, and the quilted bed comforter exquisitely appliquéd with the same print fabric. A sewing stand sat in the opposite corner, and placed on its top was a piece of unfinished embroidered needlework still stretched in its hoop. Along another wall was a large ornately carved dresser with a matching oak looking glass hung above it. In an empty drawer I placed my few articles of seamen's clothing, my diary and pouch. Before closing it, I untied the pouch and removed the little wooden cross and held it. I sat on the bed and turned the cross over and over again in my hand. The smooth wood between my fingers reminded me this was all real, not a dream. Still, I feared if I shut my eyes it would all be gone when I re-opened them. I was unable to believe that I was to occupy this beautiful space. Without closing my eyes, I thanked God for this wonderful blessing.

100

Even though I hadn't yet ventured from the house, the week following my arrival sped by quickly. There was much to do and see inside. I had to familiarize myself with the regular routine, and the captain's daily schedule. Most mornings he spent down at the wharf, and when he returned he would relate the details of the ongoings there. He grumbled that the catch didn't bring as much as he had hoped.

The market had dropped more drastically than he anticipated, and the whale oil fetched only twelve dollars a barrel instead of fifty. Baleen bone brought only seventy-cents per pound, instead of two dollars. He explained the drop in the price of whale oil was caused by kerosene increasing in popularity for use as lamp oil. Although kerosene didn't burn as cleanly or as brightly, it was significantly less costly. The price for spermaceti hadn't fallen as far. It held at thirty dollars per barrel since it was still the most superior machine lubricant available.

The captain took the effects of the bad market in stride and doled out the lay due each crewman. The next day he came home with an armful of boxes and parcels, most of them for me. He brought in packages of new clothes: - two lovely frocks, one of cotton and the other of fine silk, and numerous undergarments and other coordinated accessories. Two milliner's boxes contained hats: - a wonderful green silk spoon bonnet with wide satin ribbons and a delicately woven French straw hat with white lace trim. Best of all, in another box was a pair of soft, kid-leather shoes. I was so overjoyed with these lavish gifts, I beamed and thanked him repeatedly.

The captain smiled with pleasure. "I think these are a lot more fitting than those seaman's clothes you've had to wear." He chuckled, and light glinted brightly from his blue eyes.

"Now go ahead, at least try one on and see if it fits."

I swept the packages up to my room. The dresses were exquisite. I put on the yellow day dress complete with the new shoes and bonnet. When I left the room, I couldn't believe the elegant lady looking back at me from the tall, looking glass at the end of the hall, was me! I descended the stairs and saw the captain standing thunderstruck and staring, open-mouthed. When I reached the bottom step, he held out his hand to me.

"You look ravishing, my dear," he said without taking his eyes off me. "A precious beauty."

I placed my hand in his, stepped off the stairs and curtsied graciously. Playing the part of the flirting debutante, I laughed with carefree abandon, and said, "Why thank you, sir."

When I straightened we were face-to-face; …intimately close. I could feel his breath on my lips, feel the warmth of his body inches from mine as we held each other's gaze for a long time. He was not tall, but sturdy and fit, and stout as an oak tree. Still holding my hand, he raised his other hand to my cheek and stroked it ever so lightly as if caressing the petals of a delicate flower. He squeezed my hand, then let it go. Averting his eyes, he took a step back.

"I'm sorry, Celia, I shouldn't have…, I mean, it's just, these past weeks, …I haven't been this happy since…." He trailed off and turned away. Shaking his head he added, "…In a long time."

"It's alright, Captain." I wanted to comfort him. Shamelessly, I wanted to feel his touch again. I wanted to reach out to him, but doing so would assume far too much. We were from different worlds. I couldn't take for granted that he would welcome my affection. To avoid facing rejection I replied, instead,

"I am very fond of you, as well, And being here is more wonderful than I could ever have imagined."

He looked up at me again as if he were about to say something.

I hesitated a moment, then said, "I'll serve your dinner, now. I don't want it to get cold." And I departed.

As the weeks passed, I became acquainted with a few of the captain's friends. One couple in particular, both staunch abolitionists and near-by neighbors, were Charles and Emma Jones who came to call a few days after our arrival. Charles owned two merchant ships and shared a close friendship with the captain. His young wife, Emma, only a few years my senior, was very cordial, and we soon grew very close.

Emma was quite active in the New England Freedman's Aid Society and did a lot of charitable work to help runaway slaves who had found refuge in Washington and other Union camps farther south. The society made blankets and simple but serviceable garments to send to the refugees living at the camps. I began helping her cut out pieces of fabric for the clothing. Emma also loved to read, and often while we sewed, she would talk about the book she was currently reading. She introduced me to several new books: one by Thoreau, one by Emerson and another recently written by a freed slave writing under the name of Linda Barton.

Though she didn't know the specifics of my circumstances, I'm quite sure Emma believed I was a runaway bondwoman. She constantly enlightened me to the legal, as well as the illegal ongoings concerning the situation of Negro fugitives. From her, I learned of the recent enactment of the Personal Liberty laws that severely hindered the reclamation of runaway slaves. Even before the legal ruling, though, she said, the steadfast, local abolitionists successfully protected nearly all the runaways from recapture. The captain also kept abreast of the latest news. He told me the ongoing war, by this time, had so badly crippled the South's economy and restricted travel to the North that there was little threat of a slave hunter slipping into New Bedford unexpectedly. Between Emma's updates and the captain's vigilance, going into town posed only minimal worry to me.

I had never known such pleasurable days, each one filled with new and interesting things to see and do. When Emma and I weren't sewing, we passed many enjoyable summer afternoons strolling through the village together. While we shopped for cloth or sewing thread, Emma commented on a newly-discovered writer or artist whose work had moved and impressed her. Emma was unpretentious and compassionate; and though her convictions were strong, she was open and engaging. She had not been content to live her life as a mere spectator. Several times before the war, she had accompanied Charles on his merchant ship and voyaged to England and France where he traded goods. Emma's heart was quickened by the whispers of the muses captured by certain literature, painting and music, and her enthusiasm was contagious. We both also had an inquisitiveness about the world which made for easy and stimulating conversation and further cemented our bond. Some days, the captain escorted me to town. After we completed the household errands, we browsed the book shop or the library for a while and always bought a daily newspaper before returning home.

The busy sea-faring village was a melting pot of cultures and its townspeople, as a whole, were friendly and congenial. One could not find a place more accepting of differences in skin color or customs than New Bedford, but nothing is absolute - and there were a few exceptions.

One day, as the captain and I exited the butcher shop, we overheard voices from a gaggle of women gossiping just around the corner.

"Imagine a man like the captain buying such fine dresses for that negress," said one.

"She is very light-skinned, though. Quite beautiful for a mulatto," said another, less scornful.

"But bringing her into his home to live with him. Indecent!" gibed the first and main instigator. "A young, unmarried woman. Goodness, knows what immoral things are going on in there." They all tisk-tisked in unison.

"Scandalous."

"Downright sinful, I say," said the third.

With bold strides the captain moved in their direction.

"Good afternoon, ladies," he boomed with a smile. "Shopping today?"

The three woman stared sheepishly at one another.

"I haven't seen you in church, Mrs. Whittier, so I guess you missed the minister's sermon about how gossip and slander are born from the tongue of the devil. Wouldn't your time be better spent helping a charitable cause? Maybe doing some good for our brave soldiers, instead of idly gathering here on the street corner like a bunch of cackling hens?"

Taken aback in shame, they mumbled something in agreement.

"Good day, ladies," said the captain with a sardonic grin. He tipped his hat.

He returned to my side, putting his arm protectively around behind me and, like a perfect gentleman, guided me across the street. When we were out of sight of them, we both broke into fits of laughter.

The next time we were alone sewing in her kitchen, I told Emma what happened in the Square.

"Serves them right! Those old biddies! You never mind them." She huffed then laughed.

"Oh, Emma, you're such a dear! And a true friend!" I looked at her and smiled.

"Well, I've never seen Eben so cheery since…, well, since his wife died," she replied while putting a kettle on the stove for our tea.

"Your friendship has been good for him, Celia."

"I am very fond of him. He is a generous-hearted man and a caring, noble friend, …of high principles," I confided.

"He's a good man, …and he deserves happiness." She brought a cracker jar and jam to the table, and we sat to drink our cups of hot tea.

"I have something to tell *you*, too," she said, trying to keep me in suspense for a moment but unable to stop her lips from curving into a broad smile.

"Please tell! I said and chuckled at her expression.

"I'm with child!" she blurted. "I'm expecting!"

"That's wonderful!" I exclaimed.

"I thought it would never happen," she said.

"Oh, Emma, I'm so happy for you! When is it due?"

"In just under six months."

"We'll have to take a break from making these clothes soon, and start sewing things for the baby," I said.

"After waiting so long, I don't want to make any just yet. You know, …until I'm sure the baby's alright."

"Of course. I understand," I said. "There'll be plenty of time!"

"I was planning to volunteer with the Freedmen's Aid Society to be a reading teacher in one of the camps in Washington or at Arlington. Remember? I had told you about it? One of the seamstresses wanted to volunteer, too."

"Oh yes, I remember. But you can't go, now!"

"No, traveling would be out of the question for me," she answered.

"You need to make sure to get plenty of rest and keep your strength," I said emphatically.

"You might want to volunteer, though, Celia, in my place! That is, if the captain wouldn't mind. You don't have to stay more than two weeks. They'll be traveling by train, and you wouldn't be going alone."

"Maybe I might do that," I said. "I'll see what the captain says."

We continued drinking our tea and our conversation drifted again to literature.

Chapter Sixteen

The goal of this command is love, which comes from a pure heart and a good conscience and a sincere faith. (Timothy 1:5)

Emma was thoroughly taken by the works of Ralph Waldo Emerson who lived in Concord, just a little northwest of Boston. Last year Emma had attended one of his lectures and became very enthralled with his metaphysical ideas. She lent me his essays, "Self-Reliance", "Experience" and "The Over-Soul", her favorites. I don't know really why she had chosen those in particular, and maybe she did it without even knowing why herself. Perhaps she sensed an urgency in me, as if I was trying to fit half a lifetime into just a few months and absorb all that my new-found life had to offer. Maybe she recognized that my eagerness had little to do with making up for time lost and more to do with being afraid time was hopelessly slipping away, like dust through my fingers. I worried about Mama: where she might be, how to locate her. By doing nothing, I feared windows of opportunity may be closing with finality. I might later be helplessly searching for footprints that were swept smooth by the wind; or left lamenting, with guilt and regret, over bridges that had washed away - or sickened by the chill of a trail gone forever cold… I feared by doing nothing I was gambling with Providence, and it was taking over my mind.

I had found freedom and was content, but at what cost? When

you find something wonderful, the one single desire of your heart is to share it with those you love. I had to do everything I could to try to make that wish come true.

I was increasingly preoccupied, brooding and moping about the house. In the kitchen I mindlessly stirred a pot of beans that was simmering slowly on the hot iron stove. Just staring at it, I was totally absorbed in my thoughts and miles away. My diary was on the table, where I had been reading Mama's letter, over and over again.

The captain, watching me, asked, "You seem so somber, Celia. What are you thinking about?"

"I'm worrying about my mama, wondering where she is, - if she's alright. Unless I search for her, I may never see her again."

He said, "Here, leave that. Come sit out here with me. Tell me where you think she might be."

The captain took one of the rocking chairs, and I sat on a stool opposite. The night was beautiful, clear and cooler now. Breathing deeply, I could smell the sea but also something else, much more, like apple orchards, black earth and damp leaves. The faintest hint of autumn, still far off, but its scent subtle in the night air that floated in through the row of open shutters.

I had read Mama's letter to him when we first arrived in New Bedford, and now he read it, again.

"Do you have any idea where she might have headed after you were separated?" he said.

"No, only what she wrote in the letter, that she was going to try to get beyond Union lines. I guess she would have thought that to mean north of Fredericksburg."

"Hmm. News around town and in the *Daily Journal* says that area had seen a lot of the fighting in the past months; not recently, though. The Union seems to have control of the east there and even to the south, and they have steadily held the Confederates to their west. If she made it past the line, Union soldiers may have found her and sent her to a refugee camp farther north. I heard that the Union has commandeered escaped slaves as prisoners of war, not as captives - just so the Confederates can't seize them and take them back to the South."

"But, Captain, I'm sure she would do whatever she could to stay out of sight and not be found. Even if she evaded capture up to now though, the more time that passes the more lost she'll be. She won't know where to go to avoid soldiers, and the more likely it is she'll be caught by the Confederates,... or worse, brought back to a plantation - maybe even killed in the process."

"Emma told me about the Union's refugee camps. An abolitionist friend of Charles' took in a family from one of the camps. They told him they were thankful they were able to leave. The conditions were deplorable. The army doesn't have enough provisions for the number of people there, and they went days without food. They were half-starved. I can't abandon my mama and just go on, not knowing. I've got to try to help her north. She can find work and a new life here, too." My shoulders slumped. I bowed my head as the tears welled up in my eyes and overflowed down my face.

"Don't cry," he said moving to the edge of his chair and leaning forward. "I don't want you to be so sad," Looking toward me, he pursed his lips tight with empathy.

Then he continued, "But you can't go into the South, now. Not unless or until the South is defeated..., It would be far too dangerous,..."

"Emma told me a way that might be safe. The Freedmen's Society is looking for volunteers to teach reading at the Washington camp and the one in Arlington. It would only be for two weeks, and I could travel by train," I said hoping he would agree.

"And if you ever got caught by the Rebels you may not make it out a second time. After all you went through to leave,…, I don't want to see that happen to you. You've clawed your way off a lee shore and made it. Do you really want to go back there again? Consider what your mother sacrificed to give you this chance at real freedom, Celia. It's plain how much she cares about you. I know you love her, too, but no matter, I don't think she would want you to cast it all away. I don't want you to do that, either."

I lowered my eyes.

"I know, you are right, and I am so indebted to you, Captain. I don't want to seem ungrateful for all you've done."

"Achh," he grunted. "You don't owe me a thing," he said humbly. "And you're certainly free to do whatever you think you must.."

"I cherish your friendship, and I don't want to leave or forsake you but…," I paused.

"I care for you, Celia," he interrupted. "And for God's sake, please, … you could be risking your bloody life…"

He sat back resolutely with one hand resting squarely on each arm of the chair. He was firm in his resolve but I knew it was his way of wanting to protect me as he had already done so many times before. I wiped my eyes with the back of my hand and raised my head.

"Venturing anywhere near the South again scares me out of my wits, but I don't know any other way to find her. My heart aches to think of her lost and alone."

There was a line drawn across my heart, as clear as the Mason-Dixon Line, and the two sides of it were warring with each other like the opposing sides of the North and South. To go, or to stay. I felt a devotion to the captain; not out of duty, but out of trust and respect. I was drawn to him - to his strength of character, his supportive concern and the warmth of his heart. Our close bond brought me a satisfying peace. Though I hadn't admitted it to myself until now, I loved him, and going away would leave half my heart wounded and raw. To go or to stay - either way I would be turning my back on someone I loved. Each choice was rooted in risk and bound by the sinewy vines of disaster and reward. Only chance would determine which would burst forth its fruit - of happiness or grief.

"I do know one thing that might do, instead," said the captain. "Captain Tilson's brother, William, is here on furlough for a couple of days more before he has to leave to report back to his camp in Virginia. He's a brigadier general. I can pay him a visit and see if he might at least find out whether your mama's there in one of those holding camps."

"Yes. Oh, yes, Captain! Could you?" I brightened. "That would be wonderful! Oh, thank you! Thank you," I said and closed my hand over his. He clasped my hand and squeezed it momentarily and smiled with affection.

"I'll see him first thing in the morning."

I knew, tomorrow, he would try his best.

We stayed a while longer, together, on the moonlit porch until the the smoky trails of the evening fog rolled in and dimmed the surrounding landscape to muted shades of gray. He talked about the progress on the *Lady Grey*'s repairs and refitting. His thoroughness and attentiveness to detail with the *Lady*'s care spoke of his love for the old ship. He also told me about a sizable merchant contract he was offered for sailing a cargo of corn and wheat to England and returning with a shipload of woolen textiles and china from Stoke-On-Trent. The trip would take only a couple of months and would pay more than half the net of the last whaling voyage. We both chuckled when he said he was "actually considering shipping cargo and giving up whaling," at least for a while.

General Tilson said at least seven contraband camps had been set up in Virginia. At the captain's request, the general promised to personally check, en-route to his command post, whether a woman fitting the description of Mama was known at Camp Wadsworth or Camp Beck. Both were located near Langley, Virginia. He could also send one of his messengers to check Camp Barker and Camp Rucker, as well. But he wouldn't be able to check Camp Todd or Springdale. Both camps were located on the confiscated Arlington estate of General Lee and both housed most of the refugee women and children, but they were too far from his route.

The captain also asked similar help from another friend, Elias Carleton, a war correspondent for the *Boston Journal*. He visited army camps for weeks at a time to interview military personnel from privates to generals. For more than a month I was hopeful but my optimism slowly withered as time went on without any communication from either the general or Mr. Carleton. Finally, a telegraph came from General Tilson, but the disappointing message read, "No information found. Not located." No message appeared from Mr. Carleton.

Chapter Seventeen

He giveth power to the faint; and to them that have no might he increaseth strength. (Isaiah 40:29)

Much of my spare time I spent reading and most of my books were by authors with inner beliefs aligned to my own. Especially, I pored over the writings of Thoreau, but like Emma, above all, I cherished the essays of Emerson. His very lifeblood flowing from the pages made me realize, his is the same blood that runs through my veins. Freely, he exposed raw his personal attempts to make sense of the world in beautiful, potently-penned prose. Eloquently, he informed me of much I didn't know and enlightened me to much I hadn't noticed. Emma said with Emerson, she was kith and kin, as if joined in a collective unconscious and kindred to a greater whole. That kind of mental connection was as personal and as powerful as physical presence. Emerson was a writer that fed my soul, as well. Other books I read, even ones I didn't like or didn't understand, gave me a lot to think about from other perspectives, but the more I read of Emerson, the closer I got to my center of balance - of equilibrium, where I could find solace and came nearer to that place of perfect order.

The captain was already familiar with Emerson's essays. We talked often about how the author believed God lived in each individual, and His truth dwelled in each of us.

"Emerson believes solitude enlightens a person because it frees them from the distractions and the opinions of the world," I said one night while we were in the library together.

"Yes," the captain agreed. "I've spent long periods of solitude at sea under little other authority but my own. I often thought those idle periods were just time wasted, but in reflecting back I realized it was often more productive than the whaling itself! In the quiet moments, you're more self-reliant and you can weigh things more independently, more objectively.... A kind of truth reveals itself, if you wait long enough. Then, it's near impossible to ignore. Maybe that's the voice of God. I guess it's always there, but sometimes it's buried so deep we turn a deaf ear to it for a while."

"According to Emerson, the closer you get to enlightenment, the more you become aligned to God. He says, each of us should heed that voice of truth that lives inside us, even when it means taking risks," I continued. I told the captain that Emerson put into words what was already written on my soul.

"That's the difficult part," he said. "Living that truth in the midst of society. It can be hard to do, sometimes, without it leading to discord. That's what has this country divided in two."

"Emerson puts it that, " 'A great man is he who in the midst of the crowd keeps, with perfect sweetness, the independence of solitude,' " I quoted from the open book on my lap.

"Very righteous words to abide by. But you also have to be willing to take responsibility for your actions," he replied. "And keep your sole focus on the voice of God. Only good can come from God. It's man who creates the bad."

Emerson's ideas were turning my confusion into a sharpening clarity. They were, to me, a lighthouse beacon, guiding me and also warning of the perils that could lead me to destruction. I had already heard that inner voice that he so often mentioned. It was that voice that made me refuse to endure a grim life forced on me by others. I had to listen for it again. Little by little, I was sifting my own golden truth from the chaos muddling my heart and the trivial and the un-important started to fall away like dross. I had to search for Mama and I shouldn't squander precious time waiting.

A week later, while we were eating dinner together, the captain seemed more quiet than usual, as if something was weighing on him. He was a man to always speak his mind and was always sure of his own mind, but this time, I felt he wanted to say something but was not quite sure how to begin. He retired to the library to browse the newspaper. After tidying the kitchen I went to sit with him. As I leafed through a book of Walt Whitman poems I asked the captain if there was anything interesting in the news, but he didn't reply. He folded the paper and placed it down on the table beside him. He inhaled audibly and rubbed his brow with his fingertips before beginning to speak.

"I have learned that life's gifts are gotten by living and by grasping the joys that it offers - not by watching them pass by the wayside. And I have something that I feel I need to say." He got up from his soft chair and did not look at me as he paced around it.

"These months we've known each other...," he said slowly.

I looked up at him as he walked to me and lifted my hands. Tucking his beard nearly to his chest, he looked down at my face as if studying it for the first time.

"Well..., you are very special to me, Celia. For a long time I've felt I had no reason for being, and I thought I would never find it again." He paused.

"But you have given it back to me. You have given my life new meaning."

"You're very special to me, too, Captain," I answered as I looked up at him.

"You don't understand...," he said trying to find the right words.

"There is no denying it any longer." Still holding my hands, he lifted me to my feet.

"I'm in love with you," he said as he embraced me. I felt him sigh, as if he had been waiting to breathe. In a quiet surge of emotion, my arms fell around him, and for a long moment he held me tightly - my head against his chest.

He put me at arm's length again. I could see his cheeks blushed red, but his eyes glistened with loving devotion.

"But if you feel no affection for me, nothing need change between us," he spoke directly and looked straight into my eyes to make sure I knew his sincerity. "Everything will be as it was, I promise you."

"But if you do care for me, in the way a wife would love a husband," he continued, "then I'm asking you to be my wife. I've fallen in love with you, Celia."

Face-to-face, still in his arms, I leaned into him and said,

"I love you, too, Eben. I have for some time."

Slowly he touched his lips to mine, ever so lightly at first; with careful tenderness, then lingering long. The sweet taste of him, warm and sensual; the intimacy, profound, dizzying, disorienting - transcending all. Rising passion heated the small spaces between our bodies until we broke ourselves from its spell.

Softly, he kissed the middle of my brow, and with adoring touch, his hand stroked my hair. I nestled my head into the crook of his neck.

A tingling flush moved up through my body like a rising warm flood water with no where to go. The captain was someone I did not want to lose.

"Of course. I would be honored to be your wife! I'm in love with you, Eben. Ever since I met you, I hoped that no matter what might lie ahead, you would be by my side. I have complete trust in you; your courage; your sureness,..." His eyes twinkled and the sides of his eyelids creased as he smiled. He looked at me in that warm, delightful way. "You've never made me ashamed of what I am, where I came from or the color of my skin. Knowing you has changed the way I feel about myself. You've given me faith in myself. You're my champion."

Still holding me, he raised my chin slightly so as to look into my eyes and soothingly, he brushed his fingers over my lips.

"But you understand there might be more hurtful prejudice to bear? Even though we'd be lawfully wed and sanctified in holy matrimony?"

I nodded and closed my eyes.

"I probably can't prevent it, but I can certainly rebuke it and harshly berate the offenders," he said firmly. "But above all, I refuse to let it stand in my way - in our way. Is that alright?" he asked.

"Yes…, Eben. It is. Remember Emerson's inner voice of truth?… I've known that voice well," I said.

"It told me slavery was wrong, and wanting freedom was right. It's telling me loving you is right. If it's not in accordance with the ideals of society and presents a new set of obstacles, so be it. I won't let that stop what I feel. Accepting someone else's truth once kept me a prisoner. My truth, led me to reach for freedom. It was what got me here and it will get me through the catty gossip of busybodies."

"I see the strength in you, my love, even if at times you don't," he chuckled.

"You are a strong and determined woman. And you are a master of self-reliance. You decide what you want, then make it happen. No one else can or should force their truth on you. Each person must follow their own inner voice."

Wishing the moments to pass slowly, I stayed folded in his arms and pressed tight against him. I clenched my teeth and bit down hard on my tongue until I tasted the copper of my own blood. I wanted to spend the rest of my days with this wonderful man, and my skin went cold at the thought of jeopardizing a future with him. But the small voice inside me was crying out not to be silenced.

118

I released myself from his hold and took a few steps to the side, and turned.

"But Eben,...," I paused. "There is something else..." I hoped I would find the right words.

"I must listen to that voice in *all* areas of my life. I would be a hypocrite if I accepted my own lies and selfishly left my mama to fend for herself. I believe she needs my help. I can't go on wondering if one day I'll wake up and find I'm not the person I took myself to be, or the person you believe I am. That person would never abandon someone they loved. Following one's truth isn't always an easy path to travel, and it often takes you to a place you don't want to go; but you know it's a place you *must* go. So I beg you, please understand that I must go south, at least to search those other camps, before I can be at peace. I would be of no good to you, or to myself, if I don't."

I took a step toward him.

"Please, Eben. I want to go with your blessing."

He looked at me with sadness, then he looked away. I knew he didn't want to let me go, but I also saw sensitivity and acceptance in his eyes. It was then that I knew he wouldn't stand in my way. He understood, as I did, that when our paths diverged months ago, the roads Mama and I had chosen may have separated us for a lifetime. He realized searching the camps might be my only chance to trace her. There may never be another opportunity to locate her before all evidence disappeared - possibly forever.

"I know, now, that I must let you do this. I don't want you to throw away your tomorrows because you're too preoccupied looking back into the past. I almost fell into that trap myself. I can see the only way you can move forward is to go south to see for yourself," he said.

"I also know part of loving someone is wanting to keep them safe, and I understand more than most, how painful it is when you aren't able to do that. You wouldn't be who you are if you left your mother behind," he continued.

119

"Go," he said, "It's alright. Go with the Freedmen's Society."

I met his reach as he clutched me to him - our connection, deep and intense. A perfect union that was as absolute and real as the solidness of his body within my arms.

It troubled him that he couldn't accompany me. He had to ready the ship for her new cargo and oversee her loading and provisioning in order to abide by his contract. I told him if Mama was hiding, she probably would not show herself to anyone but me. It was best this way.

The captain did have one request, though. He asked if I would marry him before I departed on my journey. I agreed, joyfully. He said I would be safer traveling as a married woman. Not in the matter of his trust - he trusted me completely. But as long as I was in Union territory, being a married woman would ensure me more courtesy and would make it easier to send him a message or receive bank funds, if the need arose. In the South, though, our marriage wouldn't be recognized because besides being a holy bond in the eyes of God, marriage is also a legal contract between man, woman and state. The South did not extend any state's rights to Negroes, and therefore no marriage involving a Negro could be legally binding. Although in most of the Northern states, including Massachusetts, Negroes had all state privileges offered to any white person.

The next morning, Eben called on Reverend Moulton and arranged for us to be married two days later.

Chapter Eighteen

I found him whom my soul loves. On the day of his wedding, on the day of the gladness of his heart, my beloved is mine, and I am his. (Song of Solomon)

A girl's wedding day is certainly the most thrilling day of her life. I was bubbling with excitement, and the captain was as ecstatic as I. Emma came early to help me dress and doted over me like a mother hen. Eben left with Charles and would be meeting us at the church.

"Emma," I said, laughing, "you're supposed to be slowing down, in your condition!"

"I wouldn't miss this for the world." She was animated and full of energy as she adjusted the veil around my face.

She arranged the smooth folds of my off-white satin dress, then stood back.

"You look exquisite!" she sighed. "And just in time. I think the carriage has arrived!"

The driver escorted us to the carriage, and with some assistance we got gracefully aboard. The driver took up the reins, and the carriage started the few blocks to the North Christian Church.

Inside, the church the morning light shone through the high clerestory windows with whiteness as soft and dreamy as the hushed breath of a blown kiss. I walked, as if on a cloud, through the opaline nacre that filled the space so completely that no shadow dared remain. Waiting at the altar, like a vision, was Eben. He was so handsome, in his dove-gray morning suit, waistcoat and white silk cravat. His face was jubilant - aglow. Our eyes met, and I was powerless to look away. It seemed my every step took forever, but his gaze drew me to him. I was at his side long before my body caught up.

We signed our marriage certificate and were wed in a simple ceremony. My love for Eben made me weep with joy as we bound our lives to each other. When he spoke, his eyes declared the true love he had avowed. Reverend Moulton gave us his blessing and concluded with the words, "What God has joined, let no man put asunder." Those were my sentiments exactly, and to myself I added, *what God has wrought, let not the world denounce.* At the end of the ceremony, Charles and Emma, who had been grinning at us blissfully throughout the service, fussed over us with delight.

We returned home, and the four of us were greeted at the door by Murphy and his wife, Ellen. With smiling faces and warm wishes, they ushered us into the large dining room to the wedding feast they had arranged. Platters of food covered the big oval table. A juicy, roast lamb, teeming with steaming carrots and potatoes, sat in a deep tray at the center, with two silver bowls of mint sauce beside it. Golden slices of fresh-baked cranberry bread were fanned on a plate at one end of the table, and colorful wedges of fruity sweetcakes were set evenly around a three-tiered pastry stand, at the other. And, specially ordered by the captain, were three bottles of the best, imported champagne. All four guests toasted us with crystal stems of the fizzy wine, then we all sat and ate heartily until well into late afternoon.

Afterward, when everyone had bid us farewell, and we were alone, the captain, smiling with boyish charm, said, "Come with me."

He took me by the hand and led me up the stairs, and again up a second flight into the windowed cupola at the top of the turret.

He stood behind me looking out at the horizon ablaze with a late October sunset. The sun was setting on the water in a spectacular array. Across the sky, flaming red and scorching orange spilled into heated pink and blushed chastely to rose, while waiting patiently to be joined by the edge of night.

"Isn't it magnificent?" he said.

"Such colors! It's so beautiful!" I said. "Reflecting on the water like streaks of fire."

"Nature showing all her beauty, power, and mystery in the drama of a sunset. Enough to melt the heart of even an old salt like me!" he joked and took me in his arms.

I leaned against him and relaxed into the circle of his embrace. Gently, he touched his lips to the curve of my neck, and his warm breath whispered across my face. An enrapturing shiver passed through me. Together, entwined - wrapped in each other's joy as if nothing existed beyond the walls of this small, enclosed space. The ebbing day slowly darkened to indigo like God was dimming the glim, and the stars began to decorate the heavens.

He guided me through the shadows, to the daybed on the other side of the little room. He brushed my cheek with his lips. His hands, caressing, as he slipped my dress off my shoulders. I lay back on the pillows, and he moved over me, soft and light, like a gentle rain.

"I love you, Celia," he murmured low.

"And I love you, Eben," I breathed. I surrendered to his kiss with wanton abandon and welcomed him with surging desire.

The skies opened and the rain came;
faster, harder as in a stormy torrent.

Drenching, soaking, rising.
Uninhibited desire pouring over in a cascade of long-await-
ed passion.
We were as two flowing rivers joining and mingling
in the sea.
Carried whirling and free in the deep, eddying waters.
Swirling against the tide; finding true joy and fulfillment,
as united, renewed and complete, we moved together.
Reduced into just a single vortex, to the simplest of elements;
to the one most precious; the rarefied singularity of truth,
that is love.

Chapter Nineteen

But they that wait upon the Lord shall renew their strength; they shall mount up with wings as eagles; they shall run, and not be weary; and they shall walk, and not faint. (Isaiah 40:31)

The head of the Freedmen's Aid Society was thrilled that I was willing to take Emma's place, as that meant Martha Collins, wouldn't be traveling alone. The captain purchased our train tickets, and without mentioning it to Martha, he paid the additional fare for us to have a private compartment. He worried that riding in a regular passenger car, as we continued south beyond New England, might be unwise as a few railroads segregated Negroes from white passengers and made them ride in uncomfortable baggage cars. He knew I would easily pass for white long enough to get settled into a private compartment. Eben did all he could to make certain I would be safe including giving me a healthy sum of one hundred dollars as emergency money and he made me promise to send him a telegram when we arrived - or sooner, if we had any problems enroute.

The day following the wedding, Martha and I boarded the train. We were shown to our private seats and on-schedule, and the cars began moving away from the depot. I waved to Eben from the window of the compartment. He looked down-hearted as he stood alone on the deserted platform. I missed him, desperately, even before he vanished from view. If only I was able to split myself in two. I would send one of my selves to find Mama and the other to remain with the captain.

From New Bedford to Boston, as the wheels of the train pounded their clattering rhythm along the rails and the green Massachusetts landscape sped past my window, I thought only of Eben. My mind was pulled back to last night, our first night together when as one, we floated through Paradise in a separate universe unto ourselves, protected from the world, needing nothing but each other. On the shoulders of the sweet, south wind we soared in the dizzying, rarefied, atmosphere high above the deep abyss that lay beyond the edge of oblivion. I closed my eyes and got lost in memory that had been vividly painted by every one of my senses.

My love for Eben settled in my heart long before I had admitted it to myself. Over these months, his friendship and protectiveness, his understanding, and strength of character - all endeared him to me. I delighted in his happiness and I cooked special meals for him and baked his favorite pies. When he returned from town, I always felt a warm surge of anticipation when I heard his footsteps on the kitchen stoop, and as he walked through the doorway my heart leapt with joy. The gleam in his eyes when he looked at me and smiled, made my skin tingle. I suppose, through seasons of constancy our passion may lessen, and our intimacy may become steeped by time and the weather of years; but my love for Eben is firmly planted. I can no longer imagine my life without him in it.

We reached Washington within twenty-four hours. We changed trains in New York and Philadelphia, but all went as expected. I wired Eben from the Washington depot. A soldier met us and took us, by wagon, to Camp Springdale. Inside the entrance was a large manor house and beyond were numerous smaller dwellings scattered across the endless expanse of beautiful countryside that made up the Custis/Lee estate. One section was called Springdale and the other was Camp Todd, though there was no clear boundary. All of it had been overtaken by the Union and was guarded by the guns and cannon of heavily armed Fort Albany. Groups of former slaves were gathered in the open areas around the cabins and the many makeshift tents and shelters that had been rigged wherever there was space. Most of the refugees were women and children, numbering in the hundreds. As the wagon made its way along the drive, I saw many Negro soldiers posted around the manor house which was converted into the headquarters for both camps. A soldier showed us to our rooms in one of the smaller houses closer to the refugee cabins. The rooms were clean and nicely furnished, and the soldier, very accommodating to our needs. I was anxious to explore the camp. Once we were settled, Martha and I went to the cabin the soldier told us had been turned into a schoolhouse. We would be teaching there for the next two weeks.

Other volunteer teachers from the Aid Society were in the one-room schoolhouse. The class was a group of fifteen children and an equal number of adults who were reading words that had been neatly printed in columns on a chalkboard. We introduced ourselves to the other volunteers and found most had arrived a week prior. Some would be staying as long as six weeks. They kept each class study to a half-hour so the little ones didn't get bored. Outside was another chalkboard and another gathering of children and adults who were unable to squeeze inside. They were comfortably seated on empty wooden crates and barrels. When the class began, Martha helped them follow along with the lesson as I carefully wrote each of the spelling words onto the blackboard. Afterward, Martha walked back to her room with Lydia Tefft, a friend of hers who had arrived two weeks prior, but I remained behind.

After the months I had been in New Bedford, my days on the plantation seemed a lifetime ago, but seeing these women and children dressed in the coarse, crude clothing of slaves and living in tiny dirt-floor cabins, brought my own memories of that narrow, choked oppression rushing back to me in an instant. Looking at them I, at first, wanted to turn away and retreat to my room, but their faces stopped me. They were scared. They didn't know what the future held, and they had no where else they could go. There was an uncertainty in their faces, like a low, droning anxiety that kept them together as if there was safety in numbers - so they stayed. Some of them had fled the same plantations, but others had come alone.

They clearly had very little in the way of belongings or provisions, and though they were frightened, they weren't sad. They were, surprisingly, in good spirits. They called out to me, - eager to talk to someone new. They asked me to stay and were full of questions. It was evident to them I was of mixed race. They wanted to know where I was from, and if I had been a slave, too. They admired my fine cotton dress and complimented my fashionable straw hat. I told them I lived and worked in New Bedford and left it at that, but without revealing my history, I told them all I could about living in the North.

When they were comfortable with me, I asked, "I knew someone, Daisy Green, who might be living here. I was hoping I might be able to find her." I described Mama to the women.

"Never met anyone here, like that," said one woman.

"I been here over a year and I have to say the same," said another woman and a second one agreed in concert.

"Is there another schoolhouse at the other camp?" I asked.

"Yes, Camp Todd has it's own school over there." The woman pointed in the direction away from the manor house.

"It's not far. There's more people at this camp than at Camp Todd, though" said the first woman

"But you could check. Maybe your friend 's there. We don't go over to that side too often," she added.

"I would appreciate if you could ask around. Someone else here may know of her," I said. "I would be so happy to see her again!"

128

"We'll be sure and ask around," they said. "You'll be back tomorrow to give us another lesson?"

"Yes," I smiled. "We'll continue at the same time tomorrow."

"I'll be here. I sure want to learn to read." said one of them.

"Me, to!" said another and the others agreed in unison. They looked at me with big grins. Then they left.

Over the next twelve days I taught two classes a day at Springdale and two classes at Camp Todd. The women at Camp Todd were equally as congenial but no one at either camp had seen anyone that fit the description of Daisy Green. I became increasingly discouraged. Some of these women had been living here since nearly the start of the war, and in the tight-knit community of the women's camps it would be unlikely that anyone would go unnoticed for very long.

Each day when I was through with my teaching sessions, I wandered the estate and even ventured beyond its perimeter, hoping to find Mama in one of the more remote, wooded places - but I found nothing. She just wasn't here, and it is doubtful she ever was. There were only a couple of days remaining before we were to leave for New Bedford, and I decided not to return as scheduled. I needed more time to investigate to the southeast. I would forfeit my train fare if I stayed, but I still had my emergency money to purchase a later ticket home.

The morning of the thirteenth day, I brought one of the shirt dresses we made for the refugees and a pair of the donated shoes back to my room and tied them into a small parcel with my diary and purse. In the back corner of a deep closet in the hall, I hid the small suitcase I had brought from New Bedford. When I returned to the school, I informed Martha and Lydia that I would not be taking the train with them the next day. I explained my plans had changed, and I would be staying another week to teach at the other camp. Martha had not adjusted well to rural life at Springdale with its few conveniences, and she said two weeks was all she could endure of scant, tasteless meals and stark, rustic furnishings. Lydia, too, was home-sick and missed her two children. They were both looking forward to going home.

After we said our goodbyes, I walked the short lane to the telegraph office to send a message to the captain. I trusted he wouldn't think me ungracious and thoughtless for persisting in my mission just a little longer -and I *prayed* he loved me enough to understand why. I didn't want to lose Eben from my future.

My wire read: "Please forgive me. Must check further. Will stay safe. Will return very soon. I love you. Celia."

I left the office with my parcel tucked under my arm, and walked away from the little wooden depot. I weaved my way through a shortcut between two storage buildings. The area was deserted except for two soldiers standing by a shed. As I approached by the narrow path, I heard a jeering voice say,

"Well, well, if it isn't the little nigga wench. All by her lonesome."

The voice sent icy chills up my spine, and my stomach dropped. I realized the man standing in the shadow of the shack, was Walker. I stopped, and looked hard for another exit or a way to backtrack quickly, but it was too late. My panic turned to dread.

"Oh, and look, George, she's all fancied up now, too." Without looking at the other man, Walker sneered and one side of his face wrinkled into a grotesque grimace. They were both wearing Union blues, but the uniforms were tattered and mud-stained. Each had over a week's growth of beard and they had no guns that I could see.

The other man looked at me with squinty eyes and a larcenous smirk as he eyed my parcel. But he stayed off to the side; still leaning against the building. I saw a porter hurrying across the walkway toward the depot and I shouted for help; but he was too far away to hear. The man disappeared from sight and I shrank back in dismay.

Walker cackled with at my distress, then started toward me.

"Your captain ain't here to help you, this time." Walker said. He angled closer until he blocked the alley.

"I betcha her captain bought her that fancy dress!" he called to George, then laughed.

I turned to run, but before I could move, Walker quickly snatched the parcel from my hold. My nostrils pricked from the stink of liquor that preceded him.

"What've we got stashed in here? Maybe something we might help ourselves to," he said with a snort. Holding the package in both hands, but still watching me, Walker moved back toward the other man.

"Hurry up, Walker. Let's go, before we get caught out here," the other man said more impatient than scared.

Walker yanked at the tie that wrapped the sack and the brogans fell out.

"Nothing in here but a pair of worthless shoes?" He kicked them toward me. "And this rag," he said and threw the dress. It fell to the ground and covered the shoes. "And your precious diary." He held it by its covers so that anything tucked inside would fall out. When he saw it contained no money or anything else of value he threw it toward me, and it landed at my feet. He felt inside the sack again and found my money purse.

"Ah, that's more like it!" He grinned. As he fumbled with the purse, the paper money sprung out and was strewn onto the ground. "Looky here, George, he sniggered and looked over at his cohort.

George whistled a sort of catcall and cocked his head to one side.

When Walker bent over to pick up the scattered money, I quickly picked up my diary and clothes.

"Compliments of the captain!" He hissed. He held up the half-empty purse and stuffed the other money into his pocket.

"Give me my purse! I need that money for my ticket home!" I shouted.

"Home?" he said with disdain. "That ain't your home. This is your home. You're a slave! We been gettin' good money turnin' you run-aways over to slave hunters," he barked. "Ain't that right, George?" He lunged towards me.

In his drunken state, Walker's reactions were slow, and I bolted to the right to avoid his reach. I sped past him as fast as I could. Straight into the woods I fled. My dress caught on branches and burrs, but I ran without stopping until I was so winded I might pass out. I paused for a few moments to catch my breath and I listened to make sure they were not following, - then I hurried on again.

I was deep into the shadowy forest before I slowed to a relaxed walk. The sky had become mere jagged fragments of blue scattered across a vastness of green. Sunlight dappled the dark earth, and the mossy fragrance of moist, matted leaves scented the air. The silence was disturbed only by my own muted footfalls and the warbling of birds telling their secrets to the trees. Amidst a thick stand of broom grass I changed into the homespun muslin shift and brogans and left my ruined dress in the tall reeds. Now free and unhindered, I melted into the woodland again.

Chapter Twenty

For verily I say unto you, That whosoever shall say unto this mountain, Be thou removed, and be thou cast into the sea; and shall not doubt in his heart, but shall believe that those things which he saith shall come to pass; he shall have whatsoever he saith. (Mark 11:23)

"Your spirit is great, little one and you have risked much. You have both strong love, and the courage of a brave warrior," Enapay said.

"Your search has taken you a long way. If your mother made it to the swamp she would be safe there; even from soldiers. It's avoided by travelers and everybody else except runaways 'cause it's impossible to find your way once you're inside. Not even the locals venture in more than a few hundred yards. The mouth of the old canal along the eastern rim was destroyed by the Union army back when the war started. The swamp has been left to itself ever since."

"I pray she's there. The swamp is my last hope," I replied.

We had talked for a long time. Enapay's head bowed sleepily and his breathing became louder and slower. I added a few more branches to the fire, then fetched the bedrolls from the wagon. I lay them open within the circle of warmth cast by the burning logs.

Enapay's eyes opened and as he arranged his bedding, he said, "Get some sleep. We'll reach the swamp edge by late morning, then the going will get more difficult."

"Good night, Enapay," I said and pulled the soft blanket over my shoulders.

I slept fitfully. Nightmares haunted me throughout the night. In the haze of my half-sleep, a faraway image of the captain, as if seen through the wrong end of a spyglass, appeared like a vision. But his face was turned away from me. Aggrieved, stoic, sad, frustrated? I could not tell. Maybe one, maybe all. I twisted and shifted restlessly. I longed to be near him again - to make it all right. But I could not - not yet.

The time is short now. Tomorrow, in no time at all, it would be over. All will have been decided. The time had arrived to look through the lens of truth. I will find Mama or I will not. I was shaken, unnerved as if strung hanging over an abysmal pit. The sealed envelope would be opened and its contents revealed. Unopened, possibilities existed, but once I have seen for myself, that she's not there, I could do nothing more, but accept it. The past, the present and the future converged here. The rest would be in the hands of God, alone; although I guess it always has been.

We started out early and made our way along the still-evident, but long-untrodden trail through pine barrens and fens. The landscape we crossed changed gradually to larger and more frequent patches of soft, spongy marsh that was laced with low-growing thorny vines and briars. Their claws ripped at my ankles and pierced my flesh. In the bright of the sun, dragonflies flashed their iridescence, shiny and blue, as they zippered and flitted on papery wings that crackled like the sound of dry leaves. Occasionally we had to remove deadwood, turned silver by the sun, in order to continue ahead and by late morning the narrow way had all but vanished.

Enapay stopped the wagon.

"We go through there," he said and pointed down a swale to an opening no wider than a deer path.

"But careful where you step. Lots of dangerous snakes live in this

134

wet land," he cautioned as he stepped around a coiled rattlesnake that was vibrating its tail in warning and ready to strike.

We moved slowly taking care to not damage the wagon, and Traveler obediently pushed his way, step by step, into the twined vines of the tangled woodbine. The steady horse willingly pulled the wagon through the snarled brambles, and Beau, tied to the backboard, followed faithfully. The further we walked the more waterlogged the ground became. The wet earth sucked at my shoes and a few times the wagon wheels got mired deep in the mud. We secured tow lines to the sideboards. Then Enapay and I, pulling in tandem with Beau, tugged the ropes this way and that, until Traveller could haul the wagon free.

Ahead was an expanse of turquoise sky where towering and weathered cypress trees stood like graying old men, burled and twisted. Below gnarled knees and crooked legs their feet were spread wide to anchor them deep into the boggy mud. Their branches hung heavy with dripping with moss as if they were weeping tears of malignant green. In the distance, junipers balanced precariously at the edge of a sea of oily umber. Their limbs, like crippled arms, were extended at unnatural angles as if they were relying on each other to stay standing.

Roots poked up through the mud. Some resembled sharpened stakes, pointed and menacing. Others like gravestones in a long-forgotten cemetery, leaned eerily: - lifeless, solemn and forlorn. Still more, like herds of disfigured creatures or the spawn of sinister abominations, rose up from the unholy black water and stood staring - motionless and tall.

I shook those images from my head. *Think happy thoughts*, I told myself as I moved across the strange landscape.

Ahead of me, something splashed, and I gasped. The surface of the still water dimpled. In the sunny clearing to the right, a large dark form lumbered toward the brush. Its shiny hide rolled and rippled as it bounded.

"Just a black bear," Enapay said unaffected. "It's harmless."

When we reached an open, dry hummock, Enapay stopped. We leaned against the side of the wagon that was shaded by cedars and low-limbed live oaks, and immediately the yellow flies swarmed around us in a cloud - biting as they landed. I waved my arms to keep them away.

"Let's stand in the sun." Enapay said. "They only like the shade."

He led Traveller forward into the sun and moved Beau beside him. Enapay cupped his hands and twice whistled his eagle cry. He followed it with a sound like the screeching of a hawk. From off in the distance came an answer - two eagle cries and a hawk screech. Enapay repeated his calls and again came the same responses, only much nearer this time.

To our right a bush shook subtly and with the stealth of a cat, a large Negro man appeared. He moved deftly toward us. His every sense was sharp and keen. He was instinctively watchful and innately cautious, and had the calculating and efficient manner of a wild predator. On his head was a wide-brimmed hat; - a remnant of cloth hung from the back of it and covered his neck. He wore dark pants and high leather moccasins. His broad shoulders and powerful arms were outlined by the gauzy white shirt that swaddled and draped his torso to protect him from the flies. A long, sheathed dagger was stuck under his belt, and one of his callused, work-hardened hands grasped a tall, wooden, walking stick. His face was expressionless, but recognition quickly transformed it.

"Enapay!" the man said as his face broadened into a big smile of greeting. "Welcome home!"

Enapay was beaming, "Jupiter, my friend. You look well."

"Celia, this is Jupiter. He's like a brother to me. We met as boys when I first got to the Swamp. We grew up here together," Enapay said.

"Celia," Jupiter said and gave me a tip of his hat. "Welcome t' the Great Dismal."

"Glad to meet you, Jupiter," I said managing a smile. "but this doesn't seem like a very pleasant place."

"Oh, it's not that bad. Probly takes sum gettin' used to. But I been here ma entar life," Jupiter answered with a drawl.

"We still have about a mile to go to reach the settlement," Enapay said to me. Then he asked Jupiter, "Are you going to walk with us?"

"Sho' will. You might need a hand gittin' through a few tough spots where d'mud holes 'a got a li'l deeper. Swamp, she always achangin' her face from month t' month. She can be a real trickster," he said with a chuckle.

"Thank you, Jupiter, that'd be a big help," Enapay said gratefully.

Jupiter gave us another big grin.

"Celia, you can ride in d' wagon awhile. I'll hep Enapay with th' horses." A close kinship born of many years spent together was apparent between the two friends, and happily Jupiter freely extended his goodwill to me, as well.

I climbed up onto the wagon seat - glad to be out of the muck. I got bounced, rocked and knocked about by the uneven terrain, but at least I was away from the slimy sludge and the snakes.

When we rose up onto a high, sandy knoll and the going had gotten easier, Enapay said to Jupiter, "Celia has traveled many miles looking for her mother. She thinks she might have ended up here after escaping from a plantation a ways north of here."

"A lotta runaways come heyre d'last few yars. Good chance she be 'ere," Jupiter said with sincerity.

"If you met her, I think you'd remember her," I said from the wagon. "She was branded on the side of her face with a big letter S, and she can't speak. She…,"

137

Jupiter spun around. Excitedly, he started to finish my sentence for me, "She ony make certain sounds; 'cause she got no tongue? Right?"

He started to walk toward me, but I jumped out of the wagon and ran to him.

"You know her? She's here?" I asked as I yanked on his arm and shook it in my exuberance.

"Yea, yea. I know 'er. She's here!" Enapay turned around astonished at what he heard, and the two looked at each other with happiness; then they both stared at me.

"Sho', she been here fo' a while," Jupiter said. "She's doin' fine!"

"Oh, Jupiter, My God! You've made,… I've,…." I was wide-eyed with impatience and all I could think of was running to wherever Mama was. "I can't believe it! Where is she? Please show me. Point me to where she is,… I can't wait to see her!"

"We nearly there. I take ya right to 'er, " he said. Animated, he indicated the way with his walking stick.

"Let's go!" I said as I walked ahead of them - now unmindful of the muck.

"Okay, we goin'," Jupiter said chuckling. Then he and Enapay laughed heartily. They were both happy for me.

We continued on mostly through swamp water and up over the high ridges. One looking much like the next, they rose like little lost islands.

Through the next stand of scrub several small shacks and lean-tos were visible, and seated outside of a tiny shelter made of broken planks, mud-chinked logs and bark, was Mama. She looked up at the sound of the squeaky wagon, and my skin prickled with gooseflesh. I ran to her as fast as I could go.

"Mama, Mama… Mama" I shouted in between my gasping breaths and my streaming tears.

She got up from her chair and before I was halfway to her, she began scream with pure joy.

I threw my arms around her, and she hugged me so tightly I thought I would burst.

"Oh, Mama," I said as I sobbed onto the cloth of her dress. "Thank the Lord! I found you!"

She took my head in both of her hands and looked at me. I had been only half alive, until now, when I looked up into Mama's eyes.

Inside me, is a visceral place, of unknown locus, where my cherished moments with Mama are cached like treasured souvenirs of her love.

The keeper of this mystical, murky place collects reminders of the dear and wonderful things about her that are impossible for words to describe, and each of these memories have grown roots that wrapped securely around my heart. Losing Mama ripped a deep, painful wound in that place and kept it bleeding, bleeding; never stopping. Now, the bleeding had stopped. That vital place was healed and I was whole again.

"I …love …you," she said. She actually spoke the words - slowly but very clearly! "I've …been ….practicing!" For some time, we stood together and smiled at each other through our tears.

Enapay and Jupiter had been unharnessing the horses. They left them and came to the hut and joyously cheered our reunion.

Enapay went with Jupiter to his cabin to get settled and I stayed with Mama in her little shack. The shelters were not much more than scrap wood cobbled together, and were more crude than the cabins at the plantation. All the shacks were low-roofed. They had barely enough height for standing and were hardly large enough for two people to lie head to foot in any one direction. But they kept out most of the flies and rain and the roughly built bed pallets were raised high enough off the fire-hardened dirt floor so there was little worry of having a snake crawl into your bed.

I had so much to tell Mama - all that had happened while we were apart, and of course, about Eben. I told her how Enapay had saved my life. She had a slate panel one of the maroons had fashioned for her out of a thin piece of shale, and some chalk to write with. Or I should say, to draw pictures with, since she said only one outlier was able to read. She both spoke and wrote questions about New Bedford and she had even more questions about the captain. She said whenever I talked about him, she could see in my face, how much I loved him. When I told her we were married, her eyes filled with happiness and tears of joy spilled down her cheeks. She would love the captain, I said to her, and she would love New Bedford. She would easily find work there and before long it would feel like home. I asked how she had found the Swamp. Instead of answering, she opened her diary to the pages that began the night we left the Pettigrew plantation and she held it out for me to read.

Chapter Twenty-One

From Mama's Diary

Whatsoever things are true, whatsoever things are honest, whatsoever things are just, whatsoever things are pure, whatsoever things are lovely, whatsoever things are of good report; if there be any virtue, and if there be any praise, think on these things.
(Philippians 4:8)

Sometimes you mourn the loss of someone or something before you actually lose them - before they're really gone. Just the idea of not having them near is almost too much to bear. I had already begun to miss Celia days before we left Shamrock Valley but I concealed my distress from her. My own will was at war with what I knew to be right, but deep down inside the answer was clear. I had to be strong for us both even though, without a doubt, letting go of my baby girl was the hardest thing I ever had to do.

After I was certain Celia was secured in the barrel, I slid off the wagon quietly. Staying in the shadows, I snuck back among the trees and waited. It wasn't long before the wagons started to move. I listened to their creaking and rattling as they went east down the gravel road. Their sound became more faint. Far away, the dim lantern of the lead wagon faded into the darkness, and I could hear nothing but the silent night.

I may never see her again, I had to face that, but I had made the best possible choice for my baby. I knew that in my head, but in my heart the reality of what I had done began to overwhelm me. The hopelessness, the emptiness, was too consuming for me to be concerned for my own safety. I wandered aimlessly in the gloom of the forest until I collapsed beneath the split and splintered trunk of a fallen pine that was snapped almost clean and was bent low to the ground. Beneath its drooping branches I lay. I was shattered - as broken as the dying, old tree.

A dark void circled me; slinking; stalking; waiting impatiently to smother me in its death hold and devour me like a ravenous, killing beast. How easy it would be to let it do what it does best and let my life bleed out warm and red onto the cold, wormy earth. But a tiny spark with only a jot of strength, kept it at bay. Mercifully, sleep soon overtook me. A deep, dreamless sleep, but not the kind that leaves you refreshed and renewed, just the kind that rests your bones long enough so they'll lift you up and keep you moving on.

I walked north by northeast all through the day and night and kept to the densest parts of the forest where quick cover was always close. In the early morning I came to a slow river, banked on either side with exposed ledge that jutted out from easy slopes of green. The lazy water was crystal clear and cool, and cupping my hands, I drank my fill. The peacefulness of the spot was inviting, and in the gray mist of dawn I felt invisible and safe enough to do something about the pangs of hunger that cinched my stomach. Near the river's edge I collected watercress and pond weed to eat, and when I overturned a few half-submerged rocks I found a handful of crawdads that helped to further satisfy my appetite.

Warily, I scanned the jagged rock faces as I stepped carefully along the riverbed. I paused, occasionally, to listen for any unusual sounds -

but nothing. Nothing but birds that sang cheerily and flitted from tree to tree. Nothing but the half-risen sun that glinted off the craggy cliffs and a red-tailed hawk that glided gracefully above. It hovered to cast a sharp, perceptive eye on this little piece of Eden.

As I walked higher along the bank, I noticed a dark, cavernous opening. Probably carved and sculpted by eons of wind and rain, it led between two mammoth boulders and back into the side of the rocky ridge. It would make for a perfect, concealed, resting place, I thought, at least until nightfall or, maybe longer. I climbed through the crevice. Inside the air was pleasantly cool compared to the already-hot morning air outside. I walked deeper into the narrowing purple tunnel of the dank cave and stopped. I could only make out dim silhouettes of flat-topped rocks along the walls. Beyond, the passage tapered further to a smaller, blacker slit - far too tight for anything but a tiny creature to pass through. I stood in the secret silence. Slowly, my eyes adjusted to the blackness, and as everything came into focus, I was terrified at what was before me. Two eyes were looking back at me from a space in the rock pile. I was startled and unintentionally let out a garbled shriek. Immediately the eyes moved, and up rose a shadowy form not much taller than the low mound of stone. It was a boy - a young Negro boy. We stared at each other for a few moments. His shirt and pants were worn, torn rags, but clearly had been the clothing of a slave.

"Please, shush up. Or someone'll hear," said the boy who looked as scared as I felt.

I put my hand to my mouth and nodded, then looked at him hard. He couldn't have been any more than ten or twelve years old. He got up enough courage to speak again, but still kept his distance,

"You a fug'tive, too?"

I nodded again.

"It's okay, then. You can stay heyr, long as you don't make no noise. Me and ma brotha, we leavin' today, anahow," the boy said.

I pointed to him and then motioned toward the cave entrance

to ask if his brother was out in the woods, but he didn't understand my gesture.

He said, "Why don't ya speak?"

I shook my head.

"Why not?" he asked.

I opened my mouth and showed him the stump of my tongue.

"Aw, Lordy. That awful they done that t'ya!" he said with sympathy in earnest.

Footsteps sounded on the hard-packed dirt behind me, and I quickly turned around and saw a Negro man, young, but older than the first. He held three spotted-brown fish in his large hands. He held them through the gills, but they were still alive and gulping for air.

"What you doin', Cal," he said harshly. "I tole ya to stay hid. You gonna git us found out."

"She found 'er own way in. Anyway, she a runaway, like us," said the boy.

"Yeah?" he said suspiciously as he looked me up and down. "Well, she can have the whole place, soon. We leavin' soon as it's dark."

"You come from noth or souwth?" the man asked.

I pointed in the direction I had come.

"She cain't answer, Hank. Her tongue done been cut out," the boy said solemnly.

"Huh. Sorry," Hank grunted and lowered his eyes.

"Ya hongry?" Hank asked me, kindly. "I kin share some a' this," he raised the hand that was holding the fish.

I nodded appreciatively.

"Cain't make a fire t' cook 'em, though, but they good as they are."

We sat on the earthen floor, and Hank gutted the fish with his pocket knife. When they were cleaned, he handed one to me and one to Cal. The fresh, raw fish was tasty. I shared with them the rest of the cress I had stuffed into my pockets. When we were through, I pointed

144

to the fish, then smiling, I patted Hank's hand with mine as a gesture of thanks. He returned the smile, humbly.

"You got someplace particlar you agoin'? You planned on goin' nawth, you might wanna change course," Hank said flatly.

"We aheaded that away. Thought we might git to the Union army, but the fightin' and guns and cannons skeered us away. We was thinkin' we was gonna git shot at fo' sure.

"We turn around an' are stickin' to our orignal plan. We headin' to th' Dismal Swamp. Ratha take our chances there," Hank said.

"Soldiers everwhere to the nawth, a lot, dead and a lot, alive," Cal echoed. "Did't know which way t'go an' we did't wanna run into no Confederates."

I listened intently and then took out my diary and pencil. On a page I wrote the words Dismal Swamp with a question mark. I held it up to Hank.

"We cain't read nor write," Hank answered. "I'm sorry."

So I drew a picture of tall grass, an alligator and a tree, then showed it to Hank.

"The Swamp?" he asked.

I nodded. Then pointed one way, then the other.

"You askin', where it is?"

I nodded.

"It's south. Oh, probly about four, maybe five days walking," Hank said. "Fo' a long time, we hear tales that it's been a hidin' place fo' run-aways - fo' centuries."

"We git t' ther', and we be safe," Cal added.

Hank laid back on the hard ground. Cal did the same, and both were soon asleep. I folded my diary closed and leaned back against the cave wall - alone with my thoughts and with no one to talk to but myself. How I am going to live this life that I've made? Give up, give in? Sink under the ashes of despair, …Or stay alive and survive. Love reaches,… without fearing failure,… because it *must*. That's the nature of love - the nature of my love for Celia. It had kept me going this far and would, still. I held on to the glimmer of hope that Celia and I would find each other again and to the chance that, one day, I might see my dream for her fulfilled. The dreams you dream are what keep you alive. Because of my dream, I chose to survive.

Hank awoke near dusk and roused Cal.

"Ready t' go?" he said to Cal.

I walked to where Hank stood and pointed at myself, then at him, and then toward the cave opening.

"You wanna go with us?" he asked.

I nodded.

"Well,… I ain't agonna stop ya and it ain't really right leavin' ya' here by your lonesome, anaway,…," he said - thinking out loud and looking down at the ground. "Sure. Guess it cain't hurt nothin."

"Let's get goin', then." He looked at me and grinned. Cal, now fully awake, gave me a big, wide smile.

Chapter Twenty-Two

*Though thy beginning was small, yet thy latter end should great-
ly increase.* (Job 8:7)

I closed Mama's diary and hugged her tightly.

"Mama, I could never leave you forever," I said.

She held me to her for a moment, and I understood the pain, the
heartache, she endured for my sake. I felt it there, and then it was
gone. Released, as if something, a small, cryptic, withered thing, had
flown out the window. And the sadness left her.

"I know that, Celia, but I had to let you go. You were like the
firefly: impossible to keep flickering and alive inside a jar. But let it
free, and it will live and keep its bright light glowing for all to see. I
only wanted your light to keep shining," Mama said.

She invested everything she had, and might ever have, and even
though it broke her heart, she let me go. She did it out of love, the
purest love - completely self-less and unconditional. What passed
between us, without a word being spoken, was a relaxed, sigh of
contentment, a deep breath of completion and accomplishment. Our
lives had come full circle to rest at a better place than where they
had begun.

"It's wonderful, Mama, that you can speak again," I said. "How
did you do it?"

She wrote, "When I first arrived at the Swamp, a young Negro-Shawnee, named Naywalee, offered to let me stay in her shelter until I had one of my own. Daily, we helped each other tend the gardens and the chickens, fetch water, hunt, and cook. We became very good friends as well as good workmates. Sharing our time together made our lives much better than if we had to each work alone. Most afternoons, I spent writing in my diary, and she would watch. She became intrigued by the words and the letters. She wanted to try her hand at writing them and wanted to know what the words meant. At first I held up objects and wrote simple words, but soon, we ran out of subjects. We weren't able to progress much further. Many times, she asked me to speak the sounds. She wanted so badly to learn, but I was afraid to try, and I would shake my head, *no*. She got frustrated with me because I wouldn't even attempt to speak. Early one morning she hid the head of an dead alligator under the leaves of a collard plant in the section of the garden where I would be weeding that day. When I pushed back the green leaves and saw the head staring at me, I screamed and jumped back. She ran to me. Laughing so hard she could barely stand, she picked up the severed head. She said, 'I knew you had a voice! You *can* speak!' "

Mama stopped writing and spoke, "That afternoon, I tried mouthing vowel sounds, a,e,i,o,u, and writing the letters in the dirt. Every day, I formed the sounds more clearly and confidently, and Naywalee repeated them back to me. Next, I taught her the alphabet - just a few letter-sounds a day. Eventually we put the letters together into words. She even learned to read passages from my Bible. Neither one of us were ashamed of our mistakes. We'd laugh and encourage each other to keep trying until we succeeded. We both learned at the same time. She learned to read and write, and I learned to speak again!"

Before dark, Mama lit a fire in the clearing in front of the random-ly-arranged huts. Naywalee came through the brush with three marsh hares strung over her shoulder. Proudly, Mama introduced me to her friend. We spent the rest of the afternoon talking while we cleaned the game and set it in a pot to cook over the fire.

I commended Naywalee for getting Mama to do what she had feared trying at the plantation - speaking again. Naywalee was six-teen years old and very capable of caring for herself, but still had a child-like innocence and gentleness that made me at ease with her almost immediately. I'm sure Naywalee's unassuming simplicity was what made Mama comfortable enough to find her voice, no matter how she might have stumbled with her speech, at first.

Naywalee told me she had lived in the Swamp most of her life.

"I was born into slavery," she said, "on a plantation in North Caro-lina. My mother was a negro slave and my father was a Shawnee who had been sold into slavery as a young man. My father and mother had planned to escape to the Swamp when I was grown enough to travel. From when he was a boy my father had roamed the swamp trails and knew we would not be found if we reached it. But he got sick with the smallpox and died before I was four. My mother was committed to carrying out his plan and one night, we ran away from the plantation. We headed north and then northeast following the trails he had described to her. We almost got to the marsh, but slave hunters had been alerted to our escape. They sent hounds out to track us. We could hear them baying behind us and knew they were closing fast. It was hard for my mother to run in the sinking mud. She told me to go ahead - to run as fast as I could. And to keep going. She would catch up. I ran. Far back, I could hear the crazed hounds' excited yowls and the men's hostile voices, - all of them eager for vengeance. I was terrified when I heard the vicious dogs, snarling and growling. Then I heard gun shots. My ears burned with my mother's screams. I stopped to look back. A negro man, toting a string of fish stepped out of the brush and quickly snatched me up in his arms. He told me to hold on tight and not make a sound - he'd protect me. He dropped the fish to the ground and looped the string around his hand and ran away from the voices with me in his arms - the fish dragging behind us to cover our scent. When we couldn't hear them any longer he let go of the fish and kept running until we got here. The man who rescued me was Jupiter and he's been a father to me ever since."

I knew that kind of loneliness and desolation and for a young child to live, without seeing her mother again, would be especially torturous.

"Naywalee, that is tragic. I'm sorry to have made you tell it."

"It's all right. It's been over ten years now, and I'm sure my mother's not alive."

"How do you know?" I asked.

"We found out from two other runaways from the plantation. When my mother didn't give up, she was shot by the slave hunters and torn up pretty bad by the dogs. She only lived a couple of days after they brought her back to the plantation."

"That's so sad, Naywalee," I answered with great sympathy for the burden she bore.

"I have made my peace with it; mostly because of Jupiter. Besides raising me like he would his own child, he has been an understanding and inspiring friend," she replied. Her reverence and love for him was obvious.

In the garden, I helped Naywalee gather collards, ramps, and corn to add to the rabbit stew. Her long black hair that hung past her shoulders, glistened blue in the sun. I watched her weave her way through the low rows of the young leafy greens. As she picked from the plants she bent freely, sylph-like, the way Queen Anne's lace bows gracefully to to the wind - delicate, willowy but resilient. She moved with lissome grace and the natural ease of a young doe, and her spirit sang - with sweet bell-like sounds like the clear, rolling, watery melodies of a forest wood thrush.

Though her life wasn't easy, it was a simple one - calm and unworried. Despite her misfortune, she was in harmony with her world. I was glad for her - happy she had found a place for the troubles of her past to be quietly laid to rest.

When Jupiter and Enapay arrived, we portioned the stew among us and though the evening was warm, we sat around the smoldering fire to let the smoke drive off the mosquitoes that were thick in the heavy, humid air. Everywhere, luminous swamp vapors rose from the ground and glowed an unnatural green, and in the distance foxfire glimmered like flickering ghost candles.

I was tired from traveling, and the hearty meal made me sleepy. I retired to the hut early and stretched out on my pallet. Musing in the half-light with my mind drifting and floating from one deliciously pleasing thought to another, I was high in the cupola, again tucked in Eben's arms with his body warm and close - held fast to mine. I was in New Bedford browsing books and sipping tea with Mama and Emma. I was aboard the *Lady Grey* - looking over her bowsprit at the dusky horizon and breathing the fresh, salty air. Standing on the thick planks of her sturdy deck I could feel the rush of the sea beneath my feet. But the wild sounds of the untamed soon overtook the silence of my reverie, and the night came to life. I slipped slowly into slumber to a strange lullaby: - the yip-yip of coyotes, the caterwauling of swamp leopards, the grackles of night herons, and the warbles, clicks and grunts of unknown creatures baying dissonantly around me.

My dreams hearkened to the music of the swamp and conjured visions of the feral, nocturnal landscape. In my sleepy languor, the twilight was transformed into something surreal and other-worldly.

A dark place where trees loom ominously like silhouettes and cast long purple shadows across the forest floor. Where blue mist swirls and rises, and curls its cool, damp tendrils around me, - chilling me with its embrace. The very air buzzes, vibrates. It is electric with the silvery trill of peep toads, katydid, and cicadas, and alive with a symphony of bush crickets and the baritone bellows of bullfrogs. Their choruses are unchanging. Their sounds are an echoing carillon - the chant of legions. Their music is the pulse of the wild, the ancient, and the untamed: at once unnoticed, but at the same time deafening.

Chapter Twenty-Three

Surely he cuts cedars for himself, and takes a cypress or an oak and raises it for himself among the trees of the forest. He plants a fir, and the rain makes it grow. (Isaiah 44:14)

After several days of rest, Enapay and I had regained our full vigor, and at dinner he announced that the next day, he would be making his regular stops at the fringes of the swamp. He explained to Mama and me that he traded with the freed Negroes and melungeons, and some white squatters that have long-inhabited the outer rim. They grazed their raw-boned cattle and half-feral hogs on the useless marshland and sectioned off small plots where they built makeshift shanties, not much more substantial than Mama's. Whenever they needed money for things they could not trade for or find, they hired themselves out as day-laborers and cut swamp cedar for a lumber company that made wood shingles. The lumber people made no trouble for them. They were happy to pay them in cash and asked for no names. They profited greatly from the cheap labor.

"Do you need me to go with you," I asked, - offering Enapay my help.

"No. It's safer for you to stay here. We'll saddle the horses and load the packs with what I need, and I'll leave the wagon behind. I'll be back by full dark."

"Free men live at the edge?" I asked.

Yes. Slaves who were freed or bought their own freedom. And

melungeons. Some of them live deeper in the swamp, too," answered Enapay.

"What are melungeons?"

"They're mixed. Negro, Indian and White. Some were slaves, some were born in the swamp. Others just ended up here. They keep to themselves mostly, and don't want any trouble, but the regular whites around here are terrified of them. They call them the shantytown people." Enapay explained. "They're not like the wayward maroons in the southern Dismal. Those are a wild bunch. Notorious for scavenging, pillaging and raiding plantations. And they've been know to rob unsuspecting travelers… and have murdered some in the process, too," Enapay continued.

"Yeah, we don't want anna part of them ruffians," Jupiter piped in. "When I was out huntin' last month, I met up with Cal and Hank. They lives south o' here, now - a lot closer t' that rough bunch. Them maroons tole me that since th' start of th' war, mosta them outlaw swampers got together into a vigilante army and went off akillin' Confederates, lootin', an' freein' as many bond negroes as they could. They bin wreckin' havoc all over North Carolina."

"Yes, but Jupiter, to most white folks, one maroon is the same as another," Enapay contended. "They think all swampers are dangerous."

"I guess so, but that okay. It's what keeps most white folk outta here. Some others might come in along the canal, but th' swamp, she get people lost right quick. No compass work here, neither, so it ain't easy for 'em to find their ways out. When they do git out, they shore don't wanna come back in!" Jupiter chuckled. "And them rogue maroons…, they don' bother us, much. We ain't got nothin' they want," he added.

Enapay and I were sorting through the wagon and loading the pack saddles with the items he would be taking to sell. We stowed axe and hammer heads, chisels, saws, knives, nails, coarse-woven fabric, a few pots and pans, salt and gunpowder. Enapay said that those were almost the only items a maroon would ever need to buy. Usually, they didn't pay him with money, though. Instead, they traded with him. As we slid the packs back under the wagon seat, we heard movement in the brush. Coming through the canebrake was a mountain of a man - a very large negro man. About thirty-ish, a head taller than the cattails and as big around as a barrel. A small burlap sack was slung over his shoulder.

Enapay raised his head and with a look of friendly recognition, smiled and said. "Big Jake!"

The man answered through a wide grin, "I wondered when you'd be coming back t' visit, Enapay!"

"We arrived a few days ago. Celia…, this is Big Jake,"

Jake greeted me awkwardly as he put out a hand as big as a bear paw. I smiled and shook his hand.

"Big Jake lives by himself, a few miles to the east. He's of a type that prefers his own company to anyone else's," Enapay teased, and we all chuckled. "But he's as honest as he is tall and can carve wood like you wouldn't believe!"

For a moment, Big Jake lit with pride but then quickly put his sack on the back of the wagon. Clearly, he had something he was anxious to say.

"I just heard somethin' I cain't believe, Enapay! I just come from Clay's place on the outer road. He tole me the Confed'rates surrendered!" he said excitedly and turned toward me. "He sayin' the war is over!"

Mama, Naywallee and Jupiter walked to the wagon to listen to Jake's news.

"How does he know?" Enapay asked.

155

Big Jake was so stirred, he couldn't seem to talk fast enough.

"I don't take no chances venturin' outside the Dismal, so I didn't see 'em myself. But Clay said the road's full of soldiers going home, and they tole 'im. He went down to the store at Deep Creek, and there, they said that General Lee surrendered to the North at Appomattox. A Union soldier on horseback dropped a big stack of a special two-page newspaper outside the store. The paper tells all about it. The storekeeper was reading it out loud, to ever'body," said Jake excitedly.

We were astounded. The lives of everyone could be changed.

"You hear anything about this?" Jake looked around at us and then at Enapay. "On your way here?"

Everyone was staring at Jake, but no one said a word until Enapay broke the silence.

"No. Through Virginia we stayed well away from sounds of gunfire and kept to the woods. Before that, I heard many different opinions about the war, from both sides. Some blamed the war on slavery, others on the South's secession. Secession, I suppose, caused Union to declare war, but the South seceded because they wouldn't give up one particular right - the right to own slaves. Either way, surrender means the end to slavery! Jack Mullins' store at Deep Creek and Clay Collins are two of my stops. I'm going there tomorrow. I'll see what I can find out."

"I hope it's true for the sake of all the Negroes still on the plantations. They'll all be free," Jake said.

Jupiter murmured in agreement.

"It's what I've been praying to hear," Mama said.

The war, its bitterness and destruction never penetrated into the Swamp. Early on, Union soldiers blew up the mouth of the swamp canal to block passage to the Confederacy who they thought might use it to transport supplies and ammunition. Otherwise the maroons had little information about the war, and it had little effect on their lives. I told them many people in Massachusetts are passionately opposed to slavery, and had taken an active role in helping to end it. But they feel the President's only goal is to re-unify the country as quickly as possible, and he is willing to do whatever is necessary to make that happen - whether or not it included putting an end to slavery. The North sees the white South as fighting to perpetuate a way of life; an old way of life. To the Confederates, losing the war would mean the passing away of the old ways. Most citizens of Massachusetts and perhaps a other states, believe it is not the way of life that is wrong, as it is grand and luxurious at least for those of privilege, but it is slavery that is wrong. The comfort and glory of the slaveowners comes at the expense of those whom have been forcibly enslaved. For slaves, laboring does not bring much in the way of reward, and working harder doesn't translate into a better life. The South defends its position by saying slavery is for the economic good of all - all except for the slaves.

"I doubt you'd find an abolitionist or anti-slavery sympathizer anywhere in the Confederacy," I said, "and sentiment in the North is, that even if the Union wins the war, change isn't going to come easily to the South. The whole economy is dependent on slave labor."

Enapay said, "Yeah. Doing away with slavery isn't going to automatically guarantee the beginning of freedom for the slaves. Attitudes and opinions just don't change that fast."

"I've lived in the Swamp so long already," said Jake, "I'm not sure I'd leave anyway. I'm used to it here, and I like what I'm used to."

"I understand that, Jake," said Jupiter. "Even if it *is* true, I think I'll stay just as I am for the time bein', too. But I guess we won't have t' hide scared no more!"

"Well, let's see what's in your sack, there, Jake," Enapay said - lightening the mood.

"I stopped by figuring I'd leave these for you, Enapay. But now that you're here…"

Along the ledge of the wagon he started placing the most handsome figures of animals I had ever seen. From scraps of hardwood timber, were all the animals of the swamp carved in faultless detail. He captured the natural essence of each animal in the wonderful sculptures; their spirits as well as their postures. He told us he carved the alligator and the river otter out of swamp juniper; the black bear from the dark heartwood of a black walnut branch. For the swamp cat and egret he used golden, yellow pine; and a pair of marsh hares, a blue heron and an Owl were from pieces of white cedar whose grain was richly variegated from almost-white to nut-brown.

"Jake," I said, "these are marvelous! They're works of art!"

"I told you, he was good!" Enapay chuckled.

I lifted the sculpture of the marsh hares that were posed together - crouched side-by-side. It stood about eight inches high. He had modeled them with great sensitivity and skill and captured every subtlety of the animals: - the precise curve of the ears, the delicate flare of the nostrils, the alert expression of their eyes. The rich, warm browns that ran through the woodgrain further accented the figures and the entire piece was rubbed smoother than the finest satin. I touched my fingers across the lustrous patina.

"You like that one?" asked Big Jake.

"Yes, very much. It's beautiful." I replied.

"It's yours." He gleamed.

"Really?" I looked up at him.

He nodded.

"Thank you, Jake! I will treasure it!"

Chapter Twenty-Four

*You have not given me into the hands of the enemy but have set
my feet in a spacious place.* (Psalm 31:8)

Enapay arose at sunrise and saddled Traveller and Beau. I helped
him secure the packs to the two horses, then he rode away. He was
gone all day and returned a short while before sundown.

Four of us met him at the edge of the yard to hear what he had
learned. He took a newspaper from his saddlebag and, holding it
up, turned to us.

"What Jake said is true. The South has surrendered, and there's
more!" He looked serious as he handed the newspaper to me. Jupiter, Naywalee and Mama were anxious for me to read the article to
them. We walked into the light of the fire, and I looked at the folded
paper. The headlines were staggering.

I read aloud to the group.

GENERAL LEE HAS SURRENDERED TO THE UNION AT APPOMATTOX

After four years of grueling war, General Lee had no choice
but to surrender. Our armies were outnumbered ten to one,
and rations almost non-existent with no source for replenishment. Our soldiers fought bravely. Marching day and
night without rest, they held off the Union forces. With ad-

mirable valor, they cut through the enemy lines, but General Lee refused to sacrifice any more of the lives of our courageous men when it became painfully obvious that the outcome was not to be altered. The devices of our cruel enemy were working all too well. They have beaten us by starvation and by having an endless supply of soldiers to fill their ranks - not because they have conquered us. Grant commended General Lee and refused to take his sword from him as he said Lee was a man of honor and courage. General Lee was overpowered by numbers; he was not defeated. Lee was treated with great respect, and the documents for surrender were signed by both Generals on April 9, 1865 at the McClean House in Appomattox, Virginia.

After the first sentence, their cheering drowned out much of my recitation of the rest of the article. I quieted them and flipped the paper to the other half of the front page. As I read the big and bold headlines of the next section aloud, no one made a sound.

PRESIDENT LINCOLN ASSASSINATED
ON APRIL 14, 1865

President Abraham Lincoln was assassinated on April 14th, a dark day for the entire country. Five days after the surrender of the Confederates, President Lincoln was fatally shot in the head at the Ford Theater by actor, John Wilkes Booth, a Southerner by birth and a Union hater. He had organized a conspiracy that was to be carried out that night. Accomplices planned to kill Vice-President Johnson and Secretary-of-State Seward that same evening while they slept, and perhaps also intended an attempt on General Grant's life as he had accompanied the President to the theater. Booth succeeded in his part, but the rest of the scheme failed. Powell, one of Booth's accomplices, stabbed Secretary Seward at his home. Seward was badly wounded but survived and is recovering from his injuries. Booth's other co-conspirator, Atzerodt, ignored his instructions to assassinate Johnson. Johnson was never attacked. Vice-President Johnson was sworn-in as President of the United States on April 15. We, in the South, fear his retaliation upon us will make rebuilding our lives very difficult, and that he will cause us to suffer greatly for daring to go against the United States government."

Only five days apart, two jolting, shocking events occurred. We were overjoyed at the first, but the second one,...?

"I guess Booth was either a staunch Confederate who wanted revenge against the Union, or he figured if he put the Union government into turmoil the South might have a chance to rally," Enapay said.

"Or maybe both of those are true," I replied.

"If his plan had been successful, he might have accomplished just that!" Mama added. "There'd be no telling if the Confederates or Lee would have honored the terms of the surrender and that might have led to worse - victory for the Rebels!"

"I know that newspaper was written by a Confederate, but even outside the South General Lee is quite respected," Enapay said.

"He's considered an honorable man. I don't think he would have broken his word, but yes, the Confederates may have continued to fight without him. Though I don't know if it would have made much difference. Food's scarce. Crop fields had been set afire, and with few men home to run the farms almost nothing's been re-planted. Jack said the soldiers coming back are in a bad way. Nearly starved, and so weary they looked like walking dead men."

161

"Honorable? The leader of the Confederate Army?" Jake spurted with scorn.

"I feel as you do, Jake. I have no sympathy, whatsoever, for the Southern cause, either," said Enapay, "but Lee is fiercely devoted to his fellow Virginians. He's a Virginian first, and an American second. He felt bound by his loyalty to his deep Virginia roots. He vowed to stick by her and fight for whatever side she took. That does show more than a measure of honor."

"But Clay tole me he own a passel of slaves, himself. How's that honorable?" retorted Jake.

"It's not!" Mama responded adamantly.

Naywalee looked at Mama and wholeheartedly nodded in agreement.

"My husband showed me an article in the Boston paper that printed Lee's statement that 'Northerners were Pilgrims who founded their land on the basis of freedom, but are always found to be intolerant of the differing opinions others.' Does Lee consider the opinions of his slaves? He claims to be a devout Christian and said he left it in the hands of God to determine when slaves should be freed. I guess he got his answer," I said.

Everyone was silent.

"Did Lee, and Southerners, as a whole, feel they were being faithful to their own twisted truth?" I added.

"Yes. It seems to me that the South was fighting to keep slavery, while the North was fighting to keep the states united," said Enapay.

"What about President Johnson? What do you think he's goin' to do with the South?" asked Jupiter.

"I don't know, Jupiter. I don't know," I answered.

"And is the South going to abide by Federal direction?" Enapay interjected.

"I don't think much of anythin's goin' t'change for us," added Jake.

And so began the task of reconstructing the ruin and devastation of the war. More than merely restoring the destruction done to the land and its structures, the people of the North and the South would have to establish peaceful relations with each other. My hope is that the relationship will bring peace to *ALL* compatriots of America, whether white, Negro or otherwise.

Chapter Twenty-Five

*Two are better than one because they have a good reward for
their labour. For if they fall, the one will lift up the other: but
woe to him that is alone when he falleth; for he hath not another
to help him up.* (Ecclesiastes 4:9-10)

I went back into the cabin. Mama sat on the edge of the bed pallet,
and I sat beside her.

"Mama," I said as I turned to face her, "We've got to leave for
New Bedford very soon. I shouldn't be gone much longer, especially when Eben doesn't know where I am."

Her face tensed and her lips tightened. She stared at the empty
space beyond me.

"I know," she said softly.

The unspoken implications were many. She understood I didn't
want to upset my relationship with Eben any more than I had, and
by her response, I knew she didn't want me to.

"Enapay plans to start weaving his way back north the day after
tomorrow and has offered to take us with him," I said.

"Yes, he mentioned it to me, and I thanked him. It's very generous of him. He's a considerate man."

"But Celia…," she paused and took my hand. "Are you sure you
want to take me with you? Are you sure my coming to New Bed-

ford won't destroy the dream you have only just begun to live?" she asked.

"Mama, no matter what..," I squeezed her hand tightly as I spoke. "I want you with me more than anything in the world! And don't you ever doubt that!"

"I mean..., but you're married now, and you have your own life." She cast her eyes downward.

"And you can have *your* own life. You'll easily find work, make friends, ... You will have a good life, there. You were right when you told me to be aware of God's angels around me. He does make a way - a path. But when you find it, you've got to be willing to take a step of faith! That's what you helped *me* to do!" I said. I hoped with a bit of encouragement, her hesitation would disappear.

She smiled with assurance then said with enthusiasm, "Alright. We'll *both* leave with Enapay!" Her shoulders no longer slumped and her eyes brightened.

There were times when I had seen Mama enjoying moments of true happiness, but for the first time she was looking forward to the future with optimism. Like a coiled spring that had been wound tight, she was impatient with anticipation and eager to be released into motion.

I sensed Mama had always wanted to be closer to the world, in its midst, like the characters in Ada's books, but she never quite knew how she could make that wish come true. Now, she saw a way. She looked at me, and I knew doors that had been slammed shut within her, had been flung open. She was imagining her hopes and dreams as real possibilities. On the horizon was a new life - one of her own creation, one that she would compose, one that she would pilot. This time she believed freedom could be hers. And this time, we would be steering our lives into the future, together.

And now these three remain: faith, hope and love. But the great-est of these is love. (1Corinthians 13:13)

The End

Epilogue

Author's Message

The final year of the United States Civil War is the backdrop for this story, but this book was not meant to be an account of the raging battles, victories and defeats of the warring sides. It is about freedom, and the story of two slaves who answered its call when its voice, that had beckoned from afar, now came from so very near.

Most slaves had little knowledge of the war, except for that which touched them intimately. They knew only what their owners chose to tell them and information was withheld, especially when Union soldiers got nearer. But slaves knew, *firsthand*, the meaning of subjugation.

The practice of enslavement has not just been a Southern issue, and in fact is not just an American issue, - in some parts of the world it is still in practice today. Slavery is a "mankind" issue. I tried to write this book from the perspective of a human soul, - not as "Southerner" or a "Northerner" nor from the point of view of any ethnicity. It was not written to pass judgement or provide pat answers, but to raise questions and prompt reflection.

Civil War history, in particular, is a "hard history" because slavery is not a very comfortable subject to discuss. Even teachers, who deem it an important topic in understanding the past, claim it is an awkward subject to approach. But merely regurgitating a bunch of historical facts, figures and events does not constitute learning about the Civil War era, and consequently, school children often are not taught its significance *in* our past. It is necessary to know what slavery means in order to understand its evils, - and why African-American, Caucasian, and slaves of other ethnicities were willing to risk death to escape it.

Pretending slavery never happened or wiping it from our collective memory completely eliminates any possibility of learning from the past and nullifies the lives of *all* who died in the battle. What we don't know about history hurts us all. The past informs the present and in turn, forms the future. Knowing history, not denying it, has improved the present and can make what comes next even better yet.

I looked through a window in time to find answers to questions like, *"who were these people of the Civil War era?"* and *"why did they do what they did"* and to understand the hopes, dreams and fears of the people, their ethics and morals, whether held by tradition or habit; - their humanness. I did not rewrite history, but represented the culture and mindset as authentically as I was able. Each character in the story, though fictitious, is based on factual accounts of the period, but I let each speak for themselves and tell their own stories, - more from their hearts than from their heads.

Yes, indeed, horrible atrocities resulting from prejudice, injustice and oppression abounded in this era, and caused hellish hurt and pain, embarrassed with shame, placed guilt and blame. But they were not woven into the narrative to re-inflict old wounds. If that was your understanding of the story, then you missed the point of the book - and it has failed in its purpose.

Instead, like a catalyst that triggers a chemical reaction, such scenes stir and precipitate emotion that can not be easily dismissed. With more than just words, they speak directly to the soul until even the indifferent or unyielding bubble over in response and look with their hearts instead of their minds, - and redefine their own truths...., so that even blind eyes might begin to see.

Lastly, but not the least, the violence surrounding the Civil War, the most brutal and inhuman in all of history, is a painful example of what we opt for when we choose "civil war" to settle our disputes, - and is a harsh lesson of the grim cost of that choice. For Americans killing Americans, even victory is not winning, - nor does it necessarily put an end to the real conflict. Winning a war can change borders, but can it change another's ideology? Does the defeated side change its way of thinking?

Our real monument to the lives of the men who perished should be what has been transformed by their actions - a redefining of the meaning of liberty, equality and justice for all, - of the words set forth in the founding document of the United States of America. As long as our united nation continues to strive for peace, liberty and justice, and the land within our borders is never again made red with the blood of our people, no one on either side of the Civil War died in vain.

Soon to Be Released:

In the sequel to this story, the saga continues as Celia and Daisy journey through the battlefields and devastation of the brutal Civil War and press forward to sculpt their new lives in a changing United States of America.

Made in the USA
Middletown, DE
16 July 2018